About the Book

Each legendary tale in this merry collection centers on good people and Saints from countries around the world—the man with the shrewish wife who receives three wishes from Saint Brandon and uses them in a very unpredictable way, Saint Collen who outwits the wicked Son of Nudd and his Devil helpers, and young Danílo who tries to please two Saints with funny results.

Many countries are represented here. Among them are Ireland, Wales, France, Switzerland, Russia, Italy and Rumania. Dorothy Gladys Spicer has traveled to each country to collect these tales. She has read from accounts recorded long ago, and she has talked to the people to whom the stories have been handed down in regions where they originated. In many cases, she has visited the place where the tale is supposed to have happened. From this material, Mrs. Spicer has woven these warm and humorous stories about some lovable characters—and some scarier ones!

13 JOLLY SAINTS

by

DOROTHY GLADYS SPICER

illustrated by Sofia

COWARD-McCANN, Inc.   NEW YORK

INDIANAPOLIS, INDIANA

TO
MY FATHER
THE REVEREND J. LINDLEY SPICER
the first, jolliest and happiest Saint I ever knew

Library of Congress Catalog Card Number: 79-88876
Printed in the United States of America

CONTENTS

ABOUT THE 13 JOLLY SAINTS

When I was young, I once heard my elders discuss the question "What is a Saint?" I was too busy turning the matter over in my own mind, to hear what, if anything, the old ones decided. And I kept on pondering the matter, goodness knows how many years.

It wasn't until I'd read the lives of many Saints, visited their shrines and holy wells in many lands—and known some living Saints, to my way of thinking—that I made a wonderful discovery. The Saints are the Happy Ones!

It was then that I decided to write a book of *13 Jolly Saints*. For by now I knew that no one—least of all Our Lord—likes a sour face or a dour spirit. The Saints managed to keep joy and laughter in their hearts —even when traveling the bumpy road to grace. Despite loneliness, despair and fierce wrestlings with the Devil, they made the best of everything. They learned to find happiness in the wilderness, made disciples of savage beasts and praised God through all their troubles.

This way, when England's poet laureate John Masefield wrote, "The days that make us happy are the days that make us good," he must have been thinking of the Saints. For throughout the ages, that which made them happy changed the world, worked miracles of hope and brought goodness to sinful hearts.

These tales of *13 Jolly Saints* I've told in my own way. For after so many centuries, who can say this ancient Saint acted thus or thought this? All I did—after studying the old stories of scribes and monks—was to write the events as *I* think they happened.

May you enjoy reading *13 Jolly Saints* as much as I've enjoyed delving into the old and tender tales of these 13 Happy Ones.

DOROTHY GLADYS SPICER

1 THE THREE FOOLISH WISHES
(Italy)

Padre Giovanni was a generous man. Though his worldly posses-sions were few, he shared what he had with those who had less. His tumbledown hut on the road from Ostia to Rome, had a leaky roof, his larder was bare more often than not, and as for wine, if he had a whole bottle of the sour native stuff, he thought himself rich! Yet for all his poverty, the old Padre—who lived alone with his cat, Beppo—was con-tent, his hospitality unbounded and the passing wayfarer or pilgrim brought adventure to his door. "Welcome! In Christ's name, come in," Giovanni would say, his ruddy face beaming, when even a stranger came by.

And many on their way to Rome stopped at his door. Even when Padre Giovanni had naught to offer save a cup of cold water, a few plump cherries from the old tree in his small garden or only a seat in the shade, he gave with such joy that the needy, the ragged and the sick soon felt better. "The light of God's goodness shines in your heart," they said, on taking their leave. Those who could dropped a copper or two into the worn wooden bowl near the door.

When he found the coppers, the Padre was glad. "Now we can get an extra loaf, maybe two," he'd tell Beppo happily, tying the coins into his kerchief. "Dominic bakes tomorrow and we'll buy bread, along with the rich folk. Then those who come to us hungry won't go away empty

—for a while," he'd plan and stroke Beppo till he purred like a kettle.

The good Padre and the cat managed well enough. "The Lord will provide for us," the old man always said, and somehow the Lord did.

Of this the Padre had ample proof one bleak day in November, when hoar frost covered the hillside and chill winds from the Apennines swept through the village. The old man, with Beppo on his lap, shivered before his dying fire. "Never fear, little one," he said, drawing his cassock around the cat. "Come tomorrow, when the wind lessens, we'll be out cutting wood. We'll not suffer today. I've saved enough goat's milk to give you a few drops for supper. As for me, there's still a heel of good bread in the bin, and in the cellar a swallow of wine."

In spite of his cheerful words, the Padre couldn't help being anxious. For what with unwonted cold, biting winds and the time of year, no pilgrims would pass for goodness knows how long. There were no coppers in the bowl, and no likelihood of new ones finding their way there. And kind though they were, he had no right to expect the goatherd, Niccolò, and the village baker, Dominic, to give credit forever.

When a loud knock broke into his thoughts, the Padre gathered Beppo into his arms and sprang to his feet. "Mother of God!" he whispered. "A bare cupboard, and a hungry pilgrim, on such a day!"

But Padre Giovanni put on his usual smile when he flung the door wide with a hearty "Welcome, in Christ's name." What he saw was not one but *twelve* pilgrims before him, and his heart sank to the bottom of his worn sandals. For he could tell from the wan faces, ragged garments and floppy soles, they'd traveled far. What they needed was hearty food and a warm chimney corner. All he could offer was a refuge from the wind, for his fire was down to the embers.

Yet "Come in," Giovanni said hospitably to the leader of the group, a young man with a kind face and searching eyes. "My welcome is warmer than my fire," he added apologetically, as the twelve filed inside. "Still, I have enough stools for all. And I daresay, a morsel of bread dipped in wine is better than none."

"Thank you, Padre," said the young man, smiling so warmly

the room seemed less chill. "Have no fear. Whatever you have will suffice."

The old man bustled about in a dither. He pulled out stools, dusted them with his sleeve and tried to coax a few sparks from the burned-out embers. Failing that, he hurried to the larder at the rear of the hut and opened the bread bin.

When the Padre reached for the knobby end he'd been hoarding, he uttered a cry of astonishment. For what he saw were thirteen freshly baked round crusty loaves, neatly stacked, six to a side, and one on the top. "Heaven be praised," he cried, crossing himself. "Now I can feed the poor hungry ones!" He'd never seen such fine bread or sniffed anything so fragrant as these golden-brown loaves.

But as if the miracle of the bread weren't enough, when the Padre opened the cupboard—lo!—there was a big cow's milk Gorgonzolo cheese on the shelf—the kind the rich folk bought on market days. Nor was that all. Beside the cheese stood a jug of goat's milk and, in a crock, a heart-shaped butter pat. "Our Lord's sacred heart," murmured the Padre, crossing himself again.

Yet even these wonders didn't end the strange happenings. When the old man hurried back to his guests—the bread gathered up in his robe—he could scarcely believe his eyes. For the twelve he'd left shivering before a dead fire, moments earlier, now toasted their feet before brightly burning logs. "How . . . how . . . and w-who—" Padre Giovanni babbled, staring at the twelve men in turn. By now it was clear that his visitors were not ordinary men.

When the young man—the leader among them—laughed at their host's astonishment, music seemed to fill Giovanni's humble abode. "Set the table, Padre. Fetch wine from your cellar and then we shall break bread together," the young man said.

The Padre said no more. Who his guests were, whence they had come or the reason for the strange goings-on, were not his concern. He'd learned long since not to question those who stopped at his door. Just the same, as he set the rickety table for the unexpected feast, poured milk into Beppo's empty saucer, and then went to the cellar, he couldn't help wondering who his guests were.

In the cellar, the Father had another surprise. For there on the shelf, instead of one bottle holding a swallow of wine, were *seven*, filled to the brim! "There's no end to God's mercies," the good Padre murmured.

The feast that followed was merry. But before they broke bread, the old man clasped his hands, bowed his head and gave thanks for "the miracle of increase that has blessed this house." When he opened his eyes, the room seemed filled with light. Never did the Padre enjoy guests more, answer more questions about himself, or laugh so much. There never was such delicious bread, tastier cheese or butter so sweet. As for the wine, that was ambrosia. And to add to the coziness of the occasion, Beppo purred lustily, the logs crackled and sparks chased up the chimney, like fireflies in summer.

It was all too soon when the leader of the band rose and said, "Thank you, Giovanni. We must be on our way if we are to reach Rome tonight." When he clasped the Padre's hand, looked deep into his eyes and added, "God will prosper you and your work," a strange peace filled the old man's heart.

As their leader started down the road and then each of the other pilgrims, in turn, thanked the Padre and bade him farewell, he couldn't help thinking how different they were. Some were young, others old. All had gentle faces and toil-stained hands. There was one— with a grizzled beard, a red fisherman's cap and a key at his belt—who was gruff and abrupt. The last to say farewell was a beardless youth, with golden hair and the face of an angel. "Why didn't you ask our Master to give you a wish?" he whispered, grasping Giovanni's hand.

"A wish, eh? But *why?*" asked the old man.

"Because He can grant any wish in the world," the youth replied, and added urgently, "There's still time—if you want to ask, that is."

All at once the Padre's face blanched. "Do you mean He . . . He —" he asked hoarsely, trembling all over. For now, thinking of the bread, the cheese and the wine, everything fitted into place.

"Yes, He is Our Lord," said the youth. "We are His Disciples and I, John, am the youngest. But fear not, my friend. Overtake Him, ask what you will and He will grant your fondest wish—but think well, before you ask anything," he cautioned.

Without stopping to answer, the Padre gathered up his robe, ran after Our Lord and cried, "Master, Master, please may I have a wish?"

"Certainly, Giovanni," replied Our Lord, turning. "What do you wish?"

Now somehow or other, what with being so flustered, everything happening at once and no time to reflect, the old man's mind went blank. "I wish—I wish—" he stammered, twisting the end of the cord at his waist. Then his face brightened. Even he marveled at the words that poured from his lips, "I wish the bench beside my hearth to possess magic power—such power that anyone who sits down cannot rise till I say so."

His followers stared at Giovanni in stunned silence, but Our Lord said, "If that is what you want, so shall it be," and walked on with His Disciples—all except John, who now had caught up with the Padre.

"What made you ask anything so foolish?" the Youngest Disciple demanded.

"I—I don't know," confessed the Padre. "The words just—popped out."

"Well, it's not too late," John comforted. "Hurry—you can still overtake the Master. Ask something else. But think well this time."

Again the Padre didn't lose a second. He ran after the Master, asked a second wish, and then, as before, though he racked his brains, he couldn't think what to ask for. All at once, he thought of his cherry tree. Sometimes urchins went up the branches, ate the fruit and then mocked when he scolded! "I wish that anyone who climbs my cherry tree won't be able to come down—unless I give permission," he blurted.

"It shall be as you wish," said Our Lord and went on.

When the Padre turned to go home, John plucked his sleeve. "That was a silly wish"—he sighed—"but you can ask another. Only remember, 'tis the last. No man receives more than three."

As before, the Padre raced after the Master and begged, "Please, dear Lord, will you grant another wish?"

"Gladly, Giovanni, but think well," replied the Master. "This is the last."

As on the two previous occasions, Giovanni, unable to think what he wanted, knit his brow, pulled at his beard and asked what first came to mind. "I wish to win, whenever I play cards," he said glibly, though why he didn't know. He had never played cards in his life!

"Your wish is granted," said Our Lord. Giovanni mumbled his thanks, turned homeward, and the Twelve continued their journey.

John was the first to break the troubled silence that fell upon the little band. "He might have asked salvation for his own soul," he mused.

"Or redemption for this sinful world," said the Man in the Red Cap testily, toying with his key.

"He could have asked help for the Little Ones." A third Disciple sighed regretfully.

"At least, food for the needy," cried a young man with a gaunt face.

Then Our Lord spoke. "Ah, yes, my friends, you are all right," He said. "Our good Giovanni *might* have asked any of these things—or even peace for this world. But he did not. No one could tell him what to wish for. The choice had to be his. But we must wait. *How* he uses his three foolish wishes is what is important."

As for Padre Giovanni, his wishes made, he soon forgot them. For he was busier, more content, and had more strangers to look after than ever. Though life continued much as before, now he could always count on finding something in the larder. There were enough loaves in the bin, cheese in the cupboard and wine in the cellar for everyone. There were logs for the fire. And as for Beppo, *he* always had his milk, too. "Our dear Lord looks after us," his master told him, rubbing his sleek sides. "The older we grow, the better life is."

And so it seemed. Even at three score and ten years, the Padre was hardy. And what with so many stomachs to fill, sick souls to heal and strangers to send away happier than they came, no day was long enough.

That's why the Padre didn't fancy the black-hooded Stranger who appeared, one spring day, rattled bony fingers at his door and commanded, "Come with me, Giovanni, your time is up. There's nothing to fear," he added quickly. "But hurry. I'm uncommonly busy."

At first Giovanni shivered. There was something frightening about the hooded face, the hollow eyes barely seen, and the long black cloak. The old man had no wish to go with the Stranger. When he drew back from him, the Padre suddenly recalled the wishes he'd made long ago—which the Lord, in His wisdom, had granted to him. At once a daring plan took shape in his mind. If he managed right, he'd be rid of his unwelcome guest in no time at all!

"Come in, come in, Father Death," Giovanni cried with feigned hospitality and flung the door wide. "Sit down and rest on the bench by the fire while I ready myself."

Death, who was weary, sank to the bench with a sigh and watched as the old man bustled about. The Padre changed his cassock, put on his newly cobbled sandals and smoothed his white beard. At last, he called cheerfully, "I'm ready now—if you are."

When Death tried to rise, the bench on which he sat gripped him like glue. No matter how much he struggled, pulled or tugged, he couldn't get up. "What trick is this?" he bellowed so loudly the rafters shook. "Why can't I rise?"

"Because the bench is enchanted—that's why," laughed the Padre, enjoying himself hugely. "You can't get up till I say so."

"Well, now that you've had your fun, you'd better release me," said Father Death grumpily. "I have work to do."

"So have I," the Padre retorted. "I'll let you get up when you promise to go away and not return for three hundred years."

"*Three hundred years!*" shrilled Death. "How dare you? You can't—"

"Oh, yes, I can," the Padre cried, rubbing his hands in glee. "If you don't agree, you'll be sitting there, goodness knows for how long."

When he saw he had no other choice, Death grudgingly promised to go away. "But I'll be back," he growled as he slid through the door. "In three hundred years on the dot."

Thus it was that Padre Giovanni cheated Father Death and lived three centuries beyond his allotted time. And as the years came and went, he was busier, more content and less willing than ever to leave his duties on earth.

Then one beautiful spring day, when the cherries hung red and sweet on the Padre's tree, Death rapped at the door a second time. "Come with me," he ordered gruffly. "You have five minutes to get ready. And I'll not come inside," he added warily. "This time I'll wait out here."

"I can't say I blame you." The old man chuckled, his eyes twinkling. "But I can tell you're thirsty and tired. Why don't you eat cherries while you wait? This year the fruit's prime, and since I'm going with you, I'll not be needing it myself," he added wistfully.

"I'll not eat your cherries, either," Death said. "And mind you —no more than five minutes." But when the Padre left him, the fruit looked so tempting that his throat, all at once, felt dry and parched.

The Padre smiled in his beard, scurried about noisily and, looking from the window, hugged himself in glee. For as he'd hoped, Death, unable to resist the cherries, ate first one, then another. Then spying the finest fruit on the highest branches, he cautiously climbed the tree. He was already halfway up when Giovanni rushed from the house. "I'm ready," he panted. "I hope I've not kept you waiting."

"Mumm-mm," mumbled Death, his mouth full of cherries. I'll be there directly." But the next instant, finding that was easier said than done, the hollow eyes beneath the hood glowed in anger. "So— you've tricked me again, have you?" he roared, beating the limb with bony hands. "Let me down at once. With so many folks waiting, how can you do this to me?"

"Because I enjoy life too much to go with you, Father Death," cried Giovanni, pleased at his guest's predicament. "You can't get down, you know, till I give the word," he added smugly. "Shall we say another three hundred years, eh?"

As before, Death sputtered, threatened, cajoled. But when the Padre showed no inclination to release him, he promised to leave. "When next I return, remember, Giovanni," he ended grimly, "there will be no time for tricks or delays."

And there wasn't. For when Father Death called the third time, he led the Padre away directly, allowing him only time to pause at the bend in the road. When he looked back at the small rickety hut where he'd lived in contentment six hundred and seventy years, tears welled into his eyes, an odd lump rose in his throat and he sighed. It was then Death spoke as a friend. "Grieve not, Giovanni. You have been busy, led a good life, and are going to Heaven. There you'll have more to do than here, life will be beautiful and without sadness. 'Ere we part, I'll show you the way."

Padre Giovanni had no idea what happened next. How he reached the narrow winding path above the stars, where he presently found himself, he didn't know. The last thing he recalled were the words, "Continue on this way, stray neither right nor left and in time you'll arrive at the Golden Gates of Paradise."

Now, sniffing the sweetness about him, delighting in the violets, primroses and golden-eyed pink tiny daisies on each side, and harkening to birdsongs, Giovanni murmured, "Who would *want* to stray from this path?" Then, feeling the new strength in his limbs, he walked on briskly.

How long he walked, the Padre didn't know, but after a while, the path twisted oddly, and he reached an abrupt turn. There he stood still, gaping, and his heart beat wildly. For off to the left, down a crooked path, loomed Hell's high Black Gates. Beyond billowed clouds of dark smoke. Cries and wails rent his heart.

But it wasn't until he saw the ugly horned Devil at a table near the gates—dealing cards for a game of Satan's Solitaire—that the Padre had his idea—an idea so desperate he moistened his lips, tightened the cord at his waist and felt his knees knock together. Then he laughed shakily. "After all, I'd not want my dear Lord to ask, when I reach Heaven, why I didn't use my third wish," he said to himself.

Without allowing himself more time to reflect, the Padre cupped hands to lips and shouted boldly, "Hallo there, Devil, *halloo-ooo-ooo*. How about a game of cards with me?"

When the Devil glanced up, and then loped toward him—goggly eyes glowing, horns erect and tail jaunty—Giovanni explained, "I'm on my way to Heaven. Once inside the gates, I'll never be able to play cards again."

"Right you are, old man," replied the Devil, slapping the Padre's shoulder, and added cordially, "I was wishing for a partner. We'll have a fine game and then you'll be on your way—if you are lucky."

By now the pair had reached the table. The Devil pulled out a stool, motioned the Padre to sit down and said with a leer, "I suppose you know Devils play for high stakes."

"So do Padres," replied Giovanni dryly.

"Hem-m, what do you propose?" the Devil asked warily, with a nervous twitch in the tail.

"My soul, of course—if you win, that is," said the Padre so matter-of-factly he amazed himself. "But if you don't—"

"*If I don't!*" Satan snortled, slapping his thigh. "As if Devils didn't always win!"

"Nevertheless, if you don't win, you'll agree to forfeit thirteen Souls for each game *I* win," said Giovanni, ignoring the interruption.

The Devil roared with laughter. "Ho, ho, ho, old man, if that's how you want it, that's how you'll get it," he cried, when able to speak. "All *I* ask is, don't whine and say I didn't warn you, when you sizzle in Hell," he added and pushed the cards toward his partner. "If you like, you may shuffle and deal," he added, his eyes flickering.

The old man smiled. And though he'd never played before, didn't know one card from another, or how to shuffle, he did so now with the greatest of ease. What was more, he won. And as for the Devil, *he* blanched, ground his teeth and lashed his tail. "You—you swindler —you cheat!" he bellowed, after he'd lost not one but seven games in a row. Then, with a howl of despair, Satan swept the cards from the table, ground them 'neath his cloven hoof and howled, "I'll not play with a pie-faced priest! I'm undone, and you've—you've—" he sobbed, breaking down completely.

But Padre Giovanni, busy toting figures in his head, paid no heed. "Let me see—that's nothing for you. But for me, seven games, at thirteen each—hem—that makes my winnings one and ninety Souls, eh, Devil?" he asked, his eyes innocent and wide.

"Y-you know it does," blubbered the Devil, his horns drooping like newly pulled weeds.

"Fetch my Souls at once," thundered the Padre. "We have far to go. And you, my friend, had best hurry. You have some explaining to the Master Devil—before you sizzle in your own fires."

Legend doesn't state what happened, after the Devil slunk through the great Black Gates, tail between legs. There were shrieks and screams—that's all we know—save that Padre Giovanni, with one and ninety poor smoke-blackened Souls limping at his heels, arrived at last at the shining Golden Gates and pounded boldly on them.

"Who's there?" called a voice from within.

" 'Tis I, Padre Giovanni," the old man replied. The next instant, when a key turned in the lock, the gates opened wide enough to let him through and a gray-bearded man in a red cap greeted him warmly. The Padre chuckled, "Why, I know you! You're one of the Disciples. The Master brought you to my house, once long ago."

"I'm Peter," replied the Man in the Cap. "Welcome to Heaven, Giovanni. Your credit is good, and we've been expecting you—lo!—these many years."

But when Peter beckoned him to enter, the Padre shook his head. "These are my friends," he said, waving to the raggle-taggle Souls, who pressed forward eagerly. "They must come in with me."

"Never!" cried the Saint and closed the gates to a slit. "Who are they? Whence do they come? Heaven has no room for the likes of them."

"No room, eh?" the Padre repeated. Then a crafty look crept into his eyes. "If I give you a message, will you deliver it to Our Lord?" he asked. "I'll wait here."

"I'll take Him word gladly," said the Saint stiffly.

"Then ask Him, please, good Saint Peter," Giovanni said, a ghost of a smile on his lips, "when He came to my door, did I ask who His friends were, where they came from, or say I had no room for such as they?"

Without replying, Saint Peter turned and hurried to his Master. Moments later, when he returned, he hung his head in shame. "Forgive me, Giovanni, I—I didn't understand," he mumbled and flung the shining gates wide. "Our Lord says your friends are as welcome to Heaven as you."

Giovanni entered, the poor tortured Souls surged after him and great was the rejoicing among the Angels. For had not their Master explained everything when He said, "Foolish though the Padre's wishes were, he turned them to good. Through them, he ministered to many, saved his own soul and released from Satan's clutches one and ninety Poor Lost Ones."

And as for Giovanni, the old folk who still tell his remarkable story say that in Heaven, what with more work to do than on earth, he was the happiest Soul in Paradise. For he no longer had to scheme and connive to gain a few more hundred years! He had all eternity before him.

2 SAINT KEVIN'S ACRE
(Ireland)

When young King O'Tool first came to Erin's throne, a right merry monarch was he. For what with the chase closer to his heart than the sweetest colleen this side of the Shannon, he hunted all day with boisterous young lords and feasted all night in their company. From sunup to sundown, he and his comrades galloped on steeds in the royal forest. The trees shook with their merriment, their jests and halloos. Life was good. Being King was the finest job in the world!

But all the while the young King made merry, his advisers shook their heads in despair. "Is the lad that wild he'll never settle down?" they asked in vexation, when he refused to give ear to problems of state. "Can he think of naught save his own pleasure?"

"Not now," said the Lord Chamberlain, pulling at his white beard. "But give the lad time. What he needs is a wife. Should he meet a beautiful young lady—by chance, mind you—fall madly in love, woo and win her, you'd see a change in our young King. With a Queen at his side, he'd settle down. He'd rule as wisely as his late father," the old man added, a crafty light in his eyes.

And the Lord Chamberlain was right, as events that followed proved. After months of conniving, he induced the King to go to a state function which the daughter of a neighboring King, the Princess Kathleen, also attended. The instant the monarch saw her lovely face, his

22

eyes never left it. He'd never seen hair of such flaming red, such sweet cherry lips or bluer, more laughing eyes. 'Twas love at first sight for young King O'Tool. And as for the Princess, she was head over heels in love with the handsome youth the moment *she* saw him.

Before many weeks wedding bells rang throughout the land. Everyone, from the stuffiest lord to the humblest cottager, rejoiced. There never was a lovelier bride than the Princess Kathleen. In her floating veil, dress with a train and the wreath of white hawthorn on her flaming locks, she looked like an angel. And as for their King, they were proud of him. With the glittering crown on his brow, his ermine-trimmed robes and his father's jeweled sword at his side, he might have been a fairy-tale King. But 'twas the love in his eyes when he looked at his bride that made his subjects feel easy. In finding her, young King O'Tool was finding himself!

For now, with his Queen—who was wise and good, as well as beautiful—to advise and encourage, the young King helped his people. No petition was too humble for the royal pair to consider. To such as could work, they gave land to raise cabbages and potatoes. They succored the needy and fed the poor. Erin still remembers the good days when King O'Tool and Queen Kathleen ruled the land.

Those happy years were finished and done long before this story begins. For when our tale opens, King O'Tool was old and forlorn. His beloved Kathleen—and also his son and heir—perished when plague swept the land.

The grief-stricken King ruled wisely and well until at last—heavy with years and crippled in limb—he took to his bed. When he rose, it was spring. The birds were nesting, primroses blooming in hedgerows, and beyond the beeches, at the foot of the garden, the lake sparkled in the sun.

But old King O'Tool, tottering and weak, felt no joy in the spring. The day he managed to hobble on a crutch to the lake and ease himself to the grassy bank, he was sorely discouraged. "Bad luck to old age," he muttered in a surge of self-pity. "I'd rather be dead and drowned in this lake than crippled and useless to everyone."

King O'Tool had scarce spoken the dismal words when a joyous "*K'wonk, honk, honk*" overhead accosted his ear. On glancing up, he saw a lone long-necked white goose with black bill, tail and feet wing straight toward him, and his jaw dropped in astonishment. When the bird swooped to the lake with majestic grace, flapped her wings noisily and then swam toward him, he reached out a hand and laughed aloud. "Aha, avourneen—my darling—" quoth he, more pleased than he cared to admit. "So—it's friends you'd be with old King O'Tool?"

"*Honk, honk,*" the goose replied, cocking a beady eye.

And from that instant, they were friends—the King and the goose. Once more life was good. King O'Tool merry and no longer so lonely he wanted to die. Everywhere he hobbled, the bird waddled behind. She tried hard to please. While he rested on the bank, she cavorted in the sky, answered when he called, and come Tuesdays and Fridays, dived for trout for her Master's dinner.

As the weeks and months passed, King O'Tool grew stronger. He almost forgot the stiffness in his legs and the creakiness in his joints. For now, with the goose to keep him company, he once more had something to live for.

But creatures, like Kings, get feeble and old in time. And when months lengthened to years—first one—then three—and finally seven— the goose grew as stiff of wing as her master of joint. When at last the poor bird was so feeble and weak she could scarce drag one foot after the other, King O'Tool again took to brooding.

"We'd both be better dead," the King said, one day, gazing in sorrow at the poor skinny creature in his arms. She was too weak to fly now. Try though she might, the most she could limp was to the eelgrass and sedges, to nip up gnats, bits of gravel, or chew a sweet root.

That's where she was—out of sight in the sedges—the day a young fellow in a tight-fitting green jerkin, a jaunty green cap and sandles laced up the leg, sauntered up. "Good day to you, King O'Tool," he said to the King, alone on the bank. "And God bless you."

The King glanced up sharply. "And how come you'd be knowing my name?" he asked, for it was easy to tell the man in the green jerkin wasn't from 'roundabout.

"Arrah, and that's my business, not yours, Sire," replied the stranger pertly. "I know many things. And how, may I inquire, is your goose?"

The King stared, for the goose was still hidden from sight. "How come you know about *her*?" he asked suspiciously.

"That, also, is my business," said the youth. "I know all about you and your goose."

"Then who are you, young man?" the King demanded, not fancying the impertinence. "By what trade do you support yourself?"

"I'm an honest man, King O'Tool," said the young fellow. "And as for trade, you might say, it's making old things better than new."

"A tinker, eh?" the King asked. "Well, as trades go, I suppose that's good as another."

"Better!" The young man chuckled, as though enjoying a joke of his own. His eyes drifted toward the sedges, whence the bird emerged, to limp to her master. "What would you say, King O'Tool, were I offering to make your goose good as new?"

"Why—why, I'd say, 'Thanky kindly, lad, and may all the Saints o' Heaven help you when it's your turn to die!' " said the King. Clasping his hands, he added wistfully, "If you did that, you'd make an old man grateful and happy to the end of his days."

"Well, supposing I did, what would you give in return for the job?" the stranger persisted.

"Wisha, lad, I'd give anything you ask," said the King, feeling a faint hope.

"*Anything*, eh?" the youth asked, his eyes boring into the King's. "Would you, for example, give me as much land as the goose flies over, the first time—after I've made her like new, that is?"

"Aye, that I would," promised the King.

"And you'd not be going back on your word—once you get what you want?" the young fellow pressed.

The old man's eyes flashed. "No, that I'd not," said he. "I'm King O'Tool. When I make a bargain, I keep it."

"Then I'll see what I can do for your bird," the young fellow said. And before the King's astonished eyes he reached for the goose,

lifted her gently by her stiff wings and exclaimed, "Oh, you poor old bag o' bones! Sure, and I'll make you finer and stronger than ever you were." So saying, he made the sign of the cross over the bird's head, tossed her into the air and watched. When she fluttered, sagged and all but dropped, he breathed into her feathers, to give her a boost.

The bird rose with a whir. Like an eagle, she mounted higher and higher, flapped her wings and then stretched out her neck. "*K'wonk, honk, honk,*" she cried, joyfully, as when King O'Tool saw her first.

And as for the old King, seeing his poor decrepit bird fly filled him with such joy he shouted, "Me darling, me pet, the light o' me eyes." Watching her course back and forth for the dear life of her, high above the green grassy slopes of the lake, King O'Tool's heart all but burst with happiness.

After a while, her test flight finished, the goose zoomed down to her master's side. "Ah, my avourneen," he crooned. Then the King stroked her strong wings, felt her new bones and ran a finger down her sleek shiny neck. "Once more, you and I shall have a fine life together," he gloated, seeming to forget the stranger.

"Hem—what about me?" asked the man in the green jerkin after a while. "Haven't you anything to say to *me?*"

"I say you're the cleverest young fellow in Erin," the King replied, not glancing up.

"And—" asked the stranger, his voice cold as ice.

"I say, 'Thank you, lad,' till I die," the King said, smiling at the bird.

"And is that *all* you have to say?" rasped the young man. "What about the land you promised if I made your goose new?"

For the first time, King O'Tool glanced up. "I say, 'Take it and right welcome you are,'" he said. "'Twere it the last acre I own in the world, I'd say you've earned it a hundred times over."

"Troth, and 'tis well, King O'Tool," said the young man, who seemed all at once to be changing. He was taller now, and his face brighter. "You're a decent God-fearing old man, who believes a bargain's a bargain. And lucky for you 'tis so," he added. "Otherwise, your old goose would never fly again, and as for you—"

"Who—who are you?" interrupted the King fearfully, for the young man's face shone with a strange radiance.

"I'm Saint Kevin," the young man said. "And I came to test you and see what sort of man you are."

"S-Saint Kevin," gasped the King, clasping his hands and sinking to his knees as best he could with his bones so creaking and sore. "May God and the Blessed Virgin forgive me for blabbering all this while with a Saint, and me mistaking him for a tinker!"

A mischievous smile quirked the corners of Saint Kevin's lips. "Och, musha, King O'Tool," he said, raising his hand in blessing. "And how might you be knowing otherwise? I came in disguise on purpose to confuse you. And now," he concluded, his voice kind and gentle, "because I've found you're a decent old man who fears God and doesn't try to wriggle out of a promise, you and your better-than-new goose shall prosper. To the end of your days, you'll live peaceful and happy."

So saying, Saint Kevin vanished. "My avourneen," murmured King O'Tool, fondly stroking the head of his goose.

Saint Kevin kept his promise. Until King O'Tool died, at the ripe old age of one hundred and seven, the Saint cared for him and his bird. And the goose looked after her master, gave him companionship and entertained him with her pretty droll ways. She seemed younger and stronger than the day they met, and the King, strange though it was, never seemed older than when the Saint left him.

Though King O'Tool and his remarkable goose died hundreds of years ago, to this day the old folk of Ireland remember the story. They still tell of an odd wedge-shaped bit of ground near a lake. " 'Tis Saint Kevin's Acre," they say proudly. "Troth, and for a good Saint o' Heaven to own a strip of Erin makes it the finest land in the world!"

3

THE BISHOP'S BELL
(Switzerland)

The first Bishop—and the Patron Saint—of Sitten, in the Swiss Valais, was the holy Théodule. He lived in the fourth century, in a palace perched like a bird on one of two hillocks around which the town sprawls. From that height the view of the countryside is splendid, the air like new wine and God seems close even to sinners. That's one reason why Saint Théodule, and the Bishops who followed him, loved the ancient town. For nigh sixteen centuries, Sitten has remained the see of the Bishops of Valais.

But pious though most of these Bishops were, none was so pious, generous—or half so brave—as "Bishop Joder," as Sitten's inhabitants, from the greatest to the least, affectionately nicknamed their Patron, Théodule. To this day, they declare, "Bishops have come and Bishops gone, but Bishop Joder was the holiest of all."

Then the townsfolk go on to tell of the keg in his palace cellar. No one knew whence the keg came, or what manner of grape produced wine of such ruby redness, aroma and delicate flavor as it contained. Yet everyone agreed there was something strange about both the keg and the wine.

When Bishop Joder filled a goblet and offered it to a beggar, stranger or ragged wayfarer at the door, he always said, "Drink this, my friend. It will bless you and give you strength."

And so it seemed, for when a man—no matter how bedraggled—walked from the palace, he seemed to stand taller, his step was brisker and more courage shone from his eye than when he arrived.

But that wasn't all. As the Bishop's scullery maid confided one day to the cook, "No matter how much his Grace draws from the keg, there is always wine left."

"And what might you expect, from one so holy as Bishop Joder?" asked the cook tartly, peering at the girl.

Time plays strange tricks on people's memories, and after fifteen hundred years they have forgotten much about Bishop Joder. But one thing everyone in Sitten, and the entire Valais, remembers to this day. That is what happened the night of his dream.

That night, when the Bishop retired, he was sorely troubled, though why he didn't know. He'd said his prayers, confessed his sins and examined his conscience a dozen times, yet he found no peace. He tossed for hours, first this side, then that. But the more he tried to sleep, the more elusive sleep was.

At last, weary and discouraged, the Saint counted backward from one hundred to one. "One hundred, ninety-seven, seventy—" he droned drearily. He'd just counted back to one for the seventh time, when he began to feel drowsy.

The Bishop drifted into uneasy slumber. It was then he beheld the white-clad Angel, with glistening wings and face like the sun. "Sleep not, Théodule," commanded the Radiant One, addressing the Bishop by his given name. "God bids you rise, journey to Rome at once and warn His Holiness, the Blessed Pope, of danger. This very night a foe seeks to take his life."

"But—but how can I get to Rome in time?" cried the Bishop, sitting up in bed. He glanced about wildly, but saw no one. The Angel had vanished. Moonlight flooded the room with eerie brightness. It was only a dream, he told himself. Yet thinking of the Holy Father banished all thought of sleep.

Dazed and confused, the Saint sprang from bed, ran to the window and peered at the moon, now bright as a golden ducat and round as a cheese. Even if the dream *were* real, how could he reach Rome and warn the Pope? "Dear Heaven, show me a way," he murmured, as the chimes in the church tower began to strike midnight.

The last stroke had barely sounded when Bishop Joder heard shrill squeals from overhead. Glancing up, his blood froze with horror. For there, silhouetted against the moon, danced three ugly Devils, with horns on their heads, leathery wings and cleft hooves on their long nimble legs. With joyous shrieks they capered, cavorted and pinched one another's tails.

Watching their grotesque antics, the Bishop's horror gave way to anger. "Have I preached so long, and so badly, Devils dare sport above our city?" he cried, his eyes flashing.

But the next instant the Bishop's face blanched. "Heaven *has* shown me a way," he whispered, moistening his lips. "May God give me strength to follow it," he added slowly, a desperate plan taking shape in his mind—a plan so daring it couldn't fail.

Though by now his heart pounded, the Bishop stuck his head from the window, cupped his hands and shouted, "Ho, you Devils up there, come here. I have work for you."

"*Work for us!*" shouted the Devils, snickering and nudging one another. Hadn't King Satan himself long ago offered honor, promotion—and seven bags of gold—to any Demon who snared the pie-faced Bishop's soul, dragged it to Hell and delivered it? With noisy chortles, eyes bulging with greed and heavy wings rattling, the swarthy fellows swooped downward and settled at the Bishop's window ledge. "What do you want, old man?" the Oldest Devil asked in a gravelly voice.

"I want to know which of you travels the fastest," replied the Bishop matter-of-factly.

"Ho ho, that's easy! *I* do," the Youngest shouted, shoving his companions aside. "I travel faster than wind in a gale."

"As if *that* were anything! shrilled the Middle Devil, poking the Youngest in the ribs. "*I* travel faster than thought."

The Oldest Devil gave his tail an impatient flick. "You call that fast?" he rasped witheringly. "I travel around the world faster than an old woman can change her mind."

"Then you're the Devil for me—if you'll do what I want," said the Bishop, struggling to keep his voice steady. And at his words, the younger Demons, knowing their prey was lost, rose in high dudgeon and flapped away into the night.

The Oldest Devil's eyes glittered. "There's nothing I'll not do— for a soul," he grated.

"Then we'll bargain," said the Bishop, with more confidence than he felt. "If you take me to Rome—to deliver a message to the Pope—bring me back and set me down, before cockcrow, on the hill below the palace, I'll give you my soul. But if not—" he went on, a crafty light in his eyes.

"If not, ha, ha," chortled the Devil, rubbing his bony hands in glee. "Why, your wretched soul's mine already, old man!"

Not heeding the interruption, the Bishop continued. "If not, you'll promise to leave Sitten forever."

The Devil scratched his head. "Yes, yes, I promise, old man. I'll set you down before cockcrow, never fear," he cried and glanced at the moon. "But if I'm to lug you all the way to Rome and back—and then all the way to Hell—there's no time to spare."

"I'll be ready at once," said the Bishop with a show of haste. "But since a bargain's a bargain—and to be sure everything's fair on both sides—we must decide about the cocks."

"Cocks, eh?" The Devil switched his tail. "What's to decide?" he demanded suspiciously.

"Before we take off, each of us must fetch his own rooster and set him, still asleep, on a high perch that overlooks the city," said the Bishop, his voice smooth as silk. "That way, when the birds crow to-gether, we'll know neither has cheated the other."

From the first, the Devil did not fancy the notion. But after he'd roared, threatened and declared Devils were the only ones to set down conditions—and the old man refused to budge unless he had his way— he gave reluctant consent to the plan. "Have it your way, for all the good it will do," the Demon snarled. "I'll fetch my cock, you fetch yours, and no tricks, mind you."

Shortly thereafter, the Bishop—now attired in his best cope and

jeweled miter—was whizzing through the air on the Devil's back. The old man smiled in his beard as he glimpsed in the moonlight Satan's black rumpled cock. There he huddled, on the broad ledge of the town wall, sound asleep.

On the other hand, the Saint's faithful pet rooster—snow-white and shining like satin—turned and twisted uneasily atop the church steeple. Fearful of tumbling and mindful of his master's whispered command, "Do not sleep, little one, do not sleep," the bird dared close but one eye at a time.

"Hold tight, Bishop," the Devil shouted over his shoulder as his leathery wings slip-slapped the air. "We'll be in Rome quicker than an old woman can decide whether to wear an old cap or a new."

And the Devil was right. For in less than no time, or so it seemed to Bishop Joder, he'd skimmed over forests, deep gorges and the highest Alpine peaks. And then, in the flick of an eyelash, he slackened his speed, dropped to earth and landed below the Pope's sleeping chamber.

"Well, here you are," chuckled Satan, helping Bishop Joder from his back. "I'll toss you through the window, stay here and, after your chitchat with the Pope, remember, I'll be waiting to take you home," he ended, his eyes round and bright as the moon.

A thin smile played over the Bishop's lips. "As if I'd be likely to forget our pact," said he.

Once the Bishop had roused the Pope, delivered his message and told how he had journeyed to Rome, His Holiness acted at once. He summoned the guards, had the palace searched and his enemy found—and thrown into a dungeon.

Then the Holy Father turned to Bishop Joder, embraced him as a son and said, "Greater love hath no man than to risk his own soul for the sake of saving another."

And because of his boundless gratitude, the Pope gave the Bishop a bronze bell of rare workmanship, to take back to his people—a bell possessed of strange properties. "It will banish evil," the good Father promised. "When the bell rings in the belfry, the sound of its voice will protect the folk of Sitten from harm." And so saying, he blessed his guest, thanked him once more and bade him Godspeed.

When the Devil discovered he was expected to take both the Bishop and the bell back to Sitten, his eyes flared and he hopped in rage. He was about to snarl that Devils weren't beasts of burden, like donkeys, when he thought better of it. Considering the richness of the soul now all but in his clutches—and the reward for its delivery—he could afford to be generous! So he hoisted the old one to his back, clutched the bell upside down, by the clapper, and warmed up his wings. "You'll not hear it ring, now or ever, mind you," said Satan meanly. "You'll be in Hell before it does."

"Unless the cocks crow," the Bishop reminded him slyly.

"The cocks, ho, ho, I'd not count on them!" The Devil chuckled, and took off in such a hurry the Bishop grabbed at his ear. And now Satan traveled back to Sitten faster than he'd come to Rome. Like a homing bird, he flapped his heavy wings and—though the moon had set, the stars vanished and his burden was great—he flew at dizzy speed high above mountains, villages and bottomless ravines.

When at last they approached Sitten, it was yet dark, the townsfolk asleep and cockcrow an hour hence. While still afar, the Devil could see the dim motionless figure of his rooster, huddled like a bundle of rags on the wall. "He's not stirred since we left," he gloated. "How's that, old man? Are you willing to admit I've won honest and fair?"

"You've not landed—yet," said the Bishop, his eyes fixed on the white blob on top of the steeple. When the blob stirred, teetered an instant and twisted this way, then that, he clasped his hands and his lips formed the soundless words, "Crow, little one, crow. Don't fail me."

And the white cock didn't fail his master. For just as the Devil wheeled, shouted with triumph and began to catapult toward earth, the creature jerked open both eyes. Then he flapped his wings, craned his satiny neck and crowed, "Cock-a-doodle-do, *Cock-a-doodle-doo*, COCK-A-DOODLE-DOO-OOO," so gustily he wakened the Devil's rooster.

And the black bird, not intending to be outdone, flapped *his* wings and crowed, "COCK-A-DOODLE-DOOO," so raucously the startled townsfolk tumbled from bed.

Meanwhile, the rage of the rooster's master, the Devil, whose hooves had all but touched earth, was dreadful. Already the Bishop had leaped from his back, and was thanking God on his knees for his deliverance, when Satan screamed, "You mealymouthed swindler—you and your white-livered cock! You've cheated me of your Soul, but I'll destroy you."

So saying, the Devil lifted the bell high in his long skinny arms, took careful aim and hurled with all his strength.

But the bell missed the Bishop's head. It shot beyond its target, dug into the earth and made a hole full seven fathoms deep. Only then did the Devil realize the magic power of the blessed bell. Uttering a yell so despairing it brought the rumpled rooster to his shoulder, he tried to escape the wrath of the awful thing. But he was too late. Even before Satan had time to spread his wings, thunder rolled through the graying sky, lightning zigzagged, and the next instant, both he and his cock lay like limp ugly rags on the ground. Amid howls, shrieks and screams for mercy, flames rose and lapped around their bodies. Smoke billowed above them. There was a smell of sulfur—and then silence— as the sun rose and light flooded the scene.

As the townsfolk poured from their houses and rushed toward the hill, they saw their Bishop, arrayed in his best miter and cope, standing beside a great hole in the earth. He stretched out his hand and they heard him say, "Arise, blessed bell. Arise, take your place and ring."

The people gaped in wonder and awe. Some sank to their knees. For now the bell rose. From seven fathoms down, it floated up and up. Only when it reached the belfry did it stop. There, wonder of wonders, it settled into a space that seemed to receive it. And then the bell chimed.

"A miracle, a miracle!" gasped the inhabitants, gazing first at the bell, then at their Bishop.

"A miracle, indeed," the old man said, his face radiant as the new-risen sun. "His Holiness, the Pope of Rome, sends you the bell. Already it has destroyed the Devil's power and delivered my soul. The bell will ward off evil and protect this town from harm."

Then the Saint went on to describe the events of the night. Beginning with his dream, the Angel's command—and the pact he, their Bishop, made with the Devil—he spared no detail, nor did he try to spare himself. "Thanks to the Pope's blessing, his holy will—and my white cock—" he concluded, "Devils never again will dance in the moonlight above Sitten."

And they never have—not, at least, for the sixteen hundred years since the events in this story took place. "Saint Joder's bell," the inhabitants of Sitten named the Pope's gift, in honor of their beloved Bishop.

"It brought luck," the townsfolk declare to this day. "In time of danger or storm, it rang of its own accord." The bell, alas, has long since disappeared. But when you ask about Sitten's first Bishop and Patron—known to the world outside as Saint Théodule—the inhabitants smile affectionately. "For many a year, he and his faithful white pet cock lived happily in the palace on the hill. Bishops have come and Bishops gone, but never was there a holier man than our Bishop Joder."

4

THE FOOLISH WOLF
(Poland)

When the world was young and animals talked and holy hermits sought God in the wilderness, Saint Stanislaus, who became Poland's great Patron, dwelt in a hut deep in the forest.

So gentle and kind was Stanislaus that all the forest creatures, from the fiercest Lion and Bear, to the lowliest Cottontail, the friskiest Chipmunk—and even the blind Mole—scratched at his door when in trouble or perplexity. One and all, they implored, "Please, Great Saint, tell us what to do," and then waited for the wise words that fell from his lips.

To the good Saint, no need was too humble, no woe too small or sorrow too insignificant to receive his attention. And because of this, the animals loved him and grew in grace.

Saint Stanislaus understood the animals so well that they generally took his advice. When they did, it was sound. But when they didn't, they rued their folly.

But beasts, like humans, alas, often are foolish, especially when young. Such was the case of the bushy-tailed Wolf, who thought he knew better than his elders. When he asked the Saint's advice, and then didn't take it, he soon discovered his dreadful mistake.

The Wolf's trouble started early one morning, when he overtook the holy man in the forest, licked his hand and fell into step with him. "What's the matter, my friend?" asked the Saint kindly, after they'd walked on some distance in silence. "Is something on your mind?"

The Wolf hesitated. Then the words tumbled out. "Yes, yes, Great Saint. I want permission to eat human flesh."

"Human flesh, eh? Don't think of it!" replied the Saint, stroking his beard. "It's not fit to eat. You'd discover it's sour as vinegar, bitter as gall and tougher than an old skinny goat."

"You must be mistaken, Great Saint," the Wolf said obstinately. "You don't know how I yearn to try it. Before I was strong enough to bring down a deer, I ate lamb and kid. They were tender and sweet. But I'm told human meat is even sweeter."

"*Who* told you?" asked the Saint suspiciously. "The flesh of a man is tasteless and tough as the sole of my sandal."

"Cousin Jackal says it's not," argued the Wolf. "He says it's sweeter than lamb and tastier than kid. After all, *he* ought to know."

"Aha, so it's Cousin Jackal, is it?" scoffed the Saint. "By this time, you ought to know better than to let him hoodwink you."

"Why *should* he lie?" the Wolf persisted.

"Because he's a shrewd cunning fellow," chuckled the Saint. "Don't you see, by lying to you, he means to keep all the kids and lambs for himself?"

"No, no, he'd not do that," the Wolf said, padding on sullenly. But, "Please, kind Saint, give your permission—just this once," he whined. "That way, I'll discover for myself how human meat tastes, whether Cousin Jackal is a liar or not, and never bother you again."

Looking down at the obstinate Wolf, the holy man realized his mind was made up and that nothing he, Saint Stanislaus, might say, would change it. Turning the matter over in his mind, he sighed deeply. It might be better, after all, to object no more, let the Beast have his way and teach him a lesson. When the Saint finally spoke, though his manner was severe and his voice sharp, a crafty smile twitched at the corners of his lips. "Since you're determined to do this horrid thing, I'll give my permission—but there's a condition," he said.

"Yes, yes, dear Saint," panted the Wolf, licking the hermit's hand. "I'll do anything you say."

"Then go at once to the crossroads, near the pond in the trees, and wait," the Saint directed. "But mind this. You're not to harm a small boy with a slate, on his way to school, or an old man with a beard, white and long as mine. The only one you can eat is a Blacksmith in a leather apron. Do you understand?" he ended sternly.

"Yes, good Saint, and thank you," cried the Wolf, jumping around with short joyous barks. Then he sped through the forest to the crossroads, ears erect, eyes bright and tail floating behind in the wind.

At the crossroads, the Wolf settled down on his haunches, peered this way, then that, and awaited his prey with ill-concealed impatience.

After what seemed seven days and nights, the Wolf heard from somewhere beyond the bend faint cracklings, rustling leaves and then running feet. "Who's there?" he called hoarsely, craning his neck.

The next instant, when a small lad with a red cap, a red muffler around his neck and a slate under his arm, tumbled into sight, the Wolf gave a disappointed snarl. "Can't you see, Mr. Wolf, I'm a boy?" shrilled the child flying past. "I'm Jes, late as usual and running all the way to school."

"Then hurry, Jes. There's no time to lose," the Wolf shouted grumpily. "A little boy's no good to me."

As the Wolf settled back once more to wait, the minutes dragged, his stomach felt like an empty sack and the forest was silent and still as a tomb. After what seemed years, his ears caught a slow dragging sound. Someone was coming! Prickling all over, the Beast stretched his muzzle, moistened his lips and rasped harshly, "Who's coming?" When there was no reply, but the dragging grew nearer, slower and then stopped altogether, he growled threateningly, "If you don't speak up, I'll tear you to bits."

When an aged man with bent shoulders, shriveled face and a long white beard presently quavered, "Whether you do or whether you don't matters little," the Wolf hung his head in shame. "Can't you see I'm an old man? I'm on my way to church, to pray for my soul—

though sometimes I think I'll not get there," the old one added and leaned heavily on his staff.

"Then God give you strength, Grandfather, and forgive me," mumbled the Wolf contritely. "I—I made a mistake. You're not the fellow I'm waiting for."

When finally the aged man shambled on, the Wolf hunched down morosely, so ravenous now he thought his stomach and spine would meet. Just when he was sure he couldn't endure the yawning emptiness another minute, he heard such a merry whistling he sprang to his feet and chortled, "At last! At last! Only a Blacksmith could make so much noise." Then, eyes fixed on the bend, the Wolf waited, his long red tongue lolling from his jaws.

When the brawny young man, wearing a leather apron—with smoke-streaked face and great grubby hands—swung into the road, the Wolf didn't have to be told he was the one he awaited. "Ho, ho, who are you?" shouted the Beast throatily.

Now to find himself all at once face-to-face with a Wolf, with needle-sharp teeth, a red licking tongue and ferocious eyes, gave the young man a bad turn. Yet, in that instant, he seemed to hear his grandfather's advice, when he was a boy, "If you're really scared, lad, don't show it, and chances are, your worst foe won't know it."

Thinking of Grandfather now gave the young man strength to flex his muscles, clench his great fist and roar boldly, "Can't you see, Wolf, I'm the lusty Blacksmith, Pavel? I shoe all the horses and oxen for miles about. But why, may I ask, are you loitering here, instead of hunting your breakfast in the forest?" he asked uneasily, for the Wolf stood there grinning in a disconcerting way.

"Because I've found it, that's why, Blacksmith." The Wolf leered, advancing a step. "I've been waiting some time for you, am hungry and intend to devour you at once."

"But why *me*?" Pavel asked, managing to keep his voice steady.

"Because Saint Stanislaus said I could eat the blacksmith in a leather apron who'd pass this way," smirked the Wolf and added, "I've never had human flesh before, and you'll do nicely—though I can't help wishing you were cleaner."

"Ho, if *that's* all that bothers you, I'll not spoil your meal—since you'll devour me anyway. I'll just wash away the soot of the forge in yonder pond, behind the trees," the Blacksmith cried. For suddenly, a cunning scheme flashed through his mind. If Saint Stanislaus had a finger in this pie, and directed the Wolf to come here and eat him, it was because the holy man counted on him, Pavel, to teach the Beast a lesson!

And as for the Wolf—who was so fussy about food—the Blacksmith's suggestion pleased *him* more than he cared to admit. "Hurry, then," he grunted, licking his chops. "You'll taste better without that muck. But no tricks, mind you. If you try to escape, you'll be sorry," he added with a chilling growl.

"I've no doubt of that!" cried the Blacksmith, hiding a grin, and he plunged through the trees. The next minute he was splashing noisily. He spattered his smirched face, washed his brawny arms and swished his big hands through the water, till the sound echoed through the trees. But that wasn't all! From an overhanging limb he cut a stout cudgel, concealed it under his leather apron and called, "I'm ready now."

When the Blacksmith scrambled back through the trees, his face and hands were clean, but still wet. "Since you're in such a hurry, perhaps you'll let me dry them on your handsome brush," he suggested slyly.

"Not that I'm comfortable when my fur's wet," said the Wolf in a peevish tone. "But since I'm eating you, I suppose I can oblige," he went on grudgingly, turned his back and waited for the Blacksmith to dry his hands.

The foolish Wolf realized his mistake too late. For no sooner had he turned than the Blacksmith seized his long tail, wrapped it three times around his wrist and then drew the cudgel from under his apron. "Take this—and *this*," bellowed Pavel, beating the Wolf till he howled for mercy. But the louder the howls, the harder the blows and the quicker the stick fell on his back. "This will teach you to yearn for Blacksmith flesh," the youth roared.

Though the Wolf screamed and moaned, pulled this way and

that and tried to wrench himself free, his efforts were vain. The Blacksmith's grip was powerful, his blows heavy and as sure as when he hammered iron on the anvil.

When at last, the Wolf lay unconscious on the road, more dead than alive, the Blacksmith tossed his stick into the bushes, dusted his hands and chuckled, "I daresay I've taught you what Saint Stanislaus couldn't. Then on to the village the Blacksmith, Pavel, went, grinning and whistling so lustily he drowned out the songs of birds in the trees.

When the Wolf came to his senses the next day, he thought he was dead. Welts and bruises covered every inch of his body, he ached all over and as for his tail—that lay in the dust like a frayed old rope. "Oh—I'm sick! Oh—how I hurt!" he moaned when he tried to rise.

How the Wolf managed to get to his feet, he never knew. But when at last he did, it was late. He moaned at each painful step.

Now when Saint Stanislaus, praying on his knees in his hut, heard the Wolf's doleful wails, he rose quickly, reached for his staff and hurried through the forest. "Forgive me, dear Lord, for interrupting my devotions," the holy man prayed. "But one of your creatures needs help."

When the Saint finally found the Wolf, the Beast was leaning against a tree, swaying dizzily and whimpering with pain. "What is the matter, my friend?" asked the Hermit. "Tell me what happened."

"Oh—how I hurt!" the Wolf wailed. "I—I'm almost dead."

The Hermit rubbed the gray head gently. "Never mind, I'm here," he comforted. "I'll take you home and care for you."

"You were right, Great Saint," the Wolf groaned, when he could say more. "Human flesh is bitter—more bitter than wormwood. To yearn for it is folly, and to eat it madness."

"Was it really so bad?" asked the Saint sympathetically.

"Yes, yes," the Beast sobbed. "Though you'd not know, for you've not tried it. But it's bad, ah, bad! Lamb is sweet and so is kid, but man's meat burns like fire. Promise me, Great Saint, you'll never speak of it again," he concluded, shuddering.

"I promise," said the Saint, smiling in his beard. "Only foolish beasts need be warned *how* bad it is. Now come with me. I'll bathe your bruises, bind up your wounds and make you well."

"Oh—" moaned the Wolf and limped through the forest at the Saint's heels.

In time, the holy man restored the ailing Wolf to health. Even his tail was handsomer and bushier than before his dreadful encounter. And soon he became a model Beast, so says the old legend. Never again did he lust for human flesh, have dealings with Blacksmiths or cause the Great Saint to regret his promise.

5 THE PROUD SAINT
(France)

Madeleine of the red-gold tresses was the only daughter of the wealthiest sheep owner in Provence, old Jacques. Her eyes were blue—bluer than forget-me-nots in spring—her skin like the snows on the Pyrénées touched by the first blush of dawn. And as for her lips, ah, were they red? Redder than cherries and ripe for kissing!

Yet, for all her delicate beauty, the girl was haughty and vain. "Madeleine the Proud," the youths called her, though there wasn't a lad within miles who didn't adore the proud willful creature.

Old Jacques adored his daughter no less than the lads round-about. For after his beloved wife died in childbirth, he lavished all his love on his infant daughter. As the years passed and she grew into dazzling young womanhood, he indulged her in every way. He quite turned her pretty head, alas, with more jewels for her fingers, pearls for her throat and chestfuls of satins and silks than a dozen princesses could wear. "My Madeleine is the most beautiful girl in all France—nay, the entire world," he declared proudly.

With this the folk of Provence agree to this day. Their Madeleine was the most beautiful girl in the world. And that's why, what with being so spoiled by a doting father, it was hard for her to humble herself, and took so long for her to become a Saint. Generations of

46

Provençal mothers have explained this to their daughters, for *la Sainte Madeleine* is the patron of young girls. "Everyone has a chance to become a Saint—even a sinner," the mothers say, and go on to piece together the fragments of the legend of Madeleine that has been told and retold in Provence for hundreds of years.

Though the beauty of Madeleine's face and form was second to none, it was her glorious hair that was the most ravishing. When she loosed her tresses, they fell, not only to her shoulders—or to her waist —but, *mais oui*, all the way to her little shapely feet.

Small wonder it was that the village lads buzzed around Madeleine as bees around wild honey. Despite her proud airs, they loved her madly and at one time or another, each knelt at her feet and begged her to wed him. But the girl only laughed, tossed her head and flirted alike with Armand and Louis, Jean and Laurent. It wasn't as if Madeleine scorned the youths. *Mais non!* She enjoyed the company of every one of them. "But I'll wed none save the fairest one—when I find him," she told them.

Still, the young men didn't give up hope. They vied, one and all, for Madeleine's favor, and she dallied with them. That's what she was doing that Candlemas Day, long ago, when the Holy Virgin passed down the lane, saw the girl in the meadow, surrounded by suitors and commanded, "Madeleine, Madeleine, come with me to Mass."

The lighthearted Madeleine glanced at her and laughed. "Fain would I come, Holy Virgin, but 'tis lonely I'd be," she said pertly. "You offer no fair youth to keep me company."

"That is where you are wrong," replied the Virgin. "Come with me and you shall know the Fairest of All."

"The Fairest of All!" Madeleine repeated, her eyes like stars, and added—haughty even to the Mother of God—"Then I'll come! But give me a little time, Holy Virgin. I must go home and array myself as a bride going forth to meet the bridegroom—for perhaps I shall wed him."

The Virgin did give Madeleine time—all the time she needed to adorn herself. When she tripped home to put on her finery, the

Holy Mother went with her and waited while the proud beauty summoned her maid.

"Fetch my gown of green brocade, with the seven-yard train," Madeleine ordered. "Bring my lace apron worked with red roses and green leaves, my green silken slippers and the necklace of pearls."

When the maid had dressed her mistress, wound a golden girdle three times around her tiny waist and brushed her hair till it fell about her like a golden mantle, she placed a golden circlet, set with rubies and diamonds, upon her brow.

"Now I am ready, Holy Mother," cried Madeleine, her cherry lips parted in a confident smile.

And, sweeping down the land behind *la Sainte Vierge*, Madeleine was so beautiful that budded snowdrops and violets blossomed, birds burst into song and furry creatures that had slept all winter crept from their holes to gaze after her.

When the girl reached the churchyard—lo!—the bells in the belfry rang in wonderment and delight. When she opened the sanctuary door, the candles on the altar lighted of their own accord, the censor swung and sweet incense filled the air.

But after this pleasant tribute to her beauty, the girl was vexed at what happened next. For as she reached a jeweled finger toward the holy water stoup, it shrank into the wall. When she genuflected before the alter, it trembled and crackled and the red wine in the chalice spilled and stained the lace cloth.

The priest, gazing upon the beautiful face, forgot the words of the Mass and the gaping choirboys the responses. The maiden regarded them, her lips curled in scorn. "Go on, Priest, say your Mass," she taunted, tossing her red-gold hair. "Chant, Choirboys, chant." But they all remained silent and still as though frozen. And turning to the Holy Mother, she cried, "Where is the Fairest One that you promised me?"

But scarce were the words out of her mouth when the Voice of the Lord thundered, "Madeleine, Madeleine, humble yourself. Humility becomes the worshiper."

"But not me," replied Madeleine. "You gave me pride as well

as beauty. I shall wear one as the other, and humble myself neither before the Lord nor before man."

The Voice spoke with sorrow. "Madeleine, why do you cling to your sin?"

A chill passed over Madeleine and suddenly she was afraid. But, "I see no sin in myself," she whispered, her voice trembling.

"Then go, repent in a grotto in the high mountains. Stay there seven years—or until you do repent—you proud willful girl," ordered the Voice, so sternly Madeleine blanched.

"No, no, Lord—not to such a far-off place." Madeleine sank to her knees and buried her face in her hands. But even as she spoke, there was an angry rumble. The candles on the altar gutted out. In the blackness that followed, she felt herself lifted and carried through the air, across deep valleys, wide rivers, a forest of pines—and then through utter darkness.

When Madeleine was able to see again, she found herself in a rock-hewn cave on a high barren hillside. Gone was her finery—the circlet set with diamonds and rubies, the green brocade gown with the seven-yard train, the golden girdle that wrapped three times around her waist. To her dismay she discovered that her red-gold hair was pulled about her body like a shepherd's mantle. And this was her only garment, for even her feet were bare. Did the Lord think to humble her spirit by humiliating her in this way? "Never! Never!" the proud girl exclaimed and burst into furious sobs.

Rocking back and forth on her knees, Madeleine felt her heart overflow first with resentment, then self-pity. Everyone had forsaken her. She'd been brought here to the wilderness to die alone in a cave—she, the most beautiful girl anywhere. Even the Holy Mother had betrayed her! She had promised her the Fairest One. What she gave was banishment!

When Madeleine ran to the entrance of the grotto and gazed in anguish at the desolate scene spread before her, she wailed with new despair, "These rocks are higher than clouds, taller than pines and more distant from my village than the end of the world."

As days, and then weeks and months, passed, Madeleine's resentment against the injustice of her plight grew. Her longing to return to her indulgent father and easy life was almost unbearable. "It's not fair," she complained, her eyes filling with angry tears. "I eat bitter herbs instead of truffles, drink water in place of wine and sleep at night on clammy stone instead of goose down!"

Thinking of nighttime, Madeleine shuddered. The nights were the worst. For besides her bed of stone, there were fearsome noises, howling wolves and ferocious growls. Sometimes, on moonlit nights, she glimpsed huge forms, glowing eyes and long pointed teeth.

And all this while, there was no shred of repentance to be found in Madeleine's heart—only the resentment that gnawed at her. The only consolation she had, at long last, was the remembrance that her unjustified punishment was to continue seven years. And however slowly, time was passing. "The Lord gave me pride," she said. "I shall keep it. 'Tis all that is left—except for my hair," and added stubbornly, "I see no sin in myself."

Even after the years—first one, then three, five, and finally seven —had dragged by, Madeleine still saw no sin in herself, felt no humility and longed only for the day that would bring her release. "When your daughter returns, what a celebration we'll have, dear Father," she planned and tried to decide which frock she'd wear on that occasion— the blue satin with lace frills at the throat, or the yellow, worked with seed pearls.

When at last the days of her penance were done, Madeleine ran from the grotto. She hurried down the steep slope and stopped only when she reached the pool below, which sparkled like a jewel amid a grove of pine trees. "Here I'll bathe away the sorrow of seven years," she cried and plunged into the water.

As Madeleine splashed, sported and swam in ecstasy, she laughed aloud. The pain of her penance vanished. Her glorious hair, floating on the water as a banner unfurled, glowed like a golden fire. When at last she lifted her arms and watched droplets trickle like diamonds through her fingers, she turned her hands, first this way, then that. "I am beautiful—beautiful," she murmured, so softly one might have imagined no one could hear.

But the Lord heard. "Madeleine, Madeleine, sinner in my sight, return to the grotto," thundered the Voice so sternly the words resounded through the forest, the trees trembled and the sky darkened. "There you shall repent another seven years—or until you learn the meaning of humility."

Madeleine blanched at the awful pronouncement, then choked in anger. Humility, indeed! As if she hadn't already learned what that was. Days and nights in a cavern alone—beasts howling without, cold rocks within, and naught save her mantle of hair to protect her from summer's heat and winter's cold!

For the first time in her vain prideful life, Madeleine found herself doubting her own judgment. Could it be she *didn't* understand humility—the kind the Voice meant? Hadn't she always said, "I see no sin in myself," and never wondered what the Lord saw amiss in her?

A strange inner prickling seized Madeleine. It wasn't repentance —for she had none. It was, rather, a curiosity. All at once she longed to discover the magic power of a word that could banish her for another seven years. Pondering the matter, her anger ebbed away. She was surprised when, after a while, she heard herself whisper, "I'll try, Lord. I'll try to understand."

Thus Madeleine returned to the grotto, set higher than the clouds, taller than pines and more remote from her village than the end of the world. And this time, though the scene was the same, her anguish great and life harsh as before, there was a difference. A gradual change came over the girl. By her willingness to try, she had taken the first step on the journey to repentance and grace.

This Madeleine realized, for the first time, the day she climbed the high rocks above the grotto to gather enough sour blackberries, stringy roots and bitter herbs for a supper. She'd wandered farther than she'd intended, dusk was closing in and she thought she'd seen a dark fearsome form lurking near a rock, when she heard faint moans from somewhere ahead.

At first, Madeleine blanched, shook with terror and stood as one rooted to earth. But when the moans continued, turned to wails and then to shrill screams of a creature in pain, she conquered her fear. Piling her scant store of food in a crevice, she clambered up the rocks in the direction of the cries, now fainter and more hopeless each moment.

How Madeleine managed to rescue the poor frightened fawn she found trapped between two rocks, its leg broken and body bruised, she didn't know. It was night when she staggered back to the grotto with the quivering creature in her arms. Owls hooted in the trees, Beasts padded on stealthy feet and each shadow concealed hidden danger. Yet the fawn's frightened moans gave her courage to stumble on. "Fear not, little one," she whispered. "I'll take care of you. No harm shall befall you."

In the days and nights that followed, Madeleine kept her promise. She nursed the fawn back to health. The day the small creature stood on wobbly legs and gazed at her with gratitude was the happiest she could remember. And when the fawn was well enough to return to the forest and refused to leave her, the girl no longer felt alone in the wilderness.

And now Madeleine, who'd never loved anything—or anyone—save herself, began to ponder the meaning of love. "It's *giving*—not taking everything—as I did from my father, who showered me with baubles and jewels, or Armand and Louis, who wanted to wed me. I never gave anything," she ended and burst into tears.

And then, thinking of love, Madeleine's thoughts turned as many times before, to the Holy Mother's promise of the Fairest One. *La Sainte Vierge* never kept it! And then for a reason she didn't understand, the girl's heart filled with longing. She bowed her head and prayed, "Make me worthy, Lord. Let me know him."

But this was not to be—not yet. For Madeleine had first to grow in grace and understanding.

As the years passed, one, and three, and finally seven, Madeleine found peace—and also friends. For she was kind, not only to her constant companion, the fawn—now grown into a large and gentle doe—but to all the birds and beasts of the wilderness. And in return for her kindness, they cared for her. The bear from whose paw she extracted a thorn brought her wild honey. The raven with the broken wing she'd sheltered until it could fly returned one day. It fluttered before her, until they reached a patch of sweet wild strawberries she had never seen. Even the ugly horned toad she'd rescued from a vulture proved his friendship by standing guard at the entrance to the grotto. Thus the years passed quickly and Madeleine learned humility from the humble creatures who surrounded her with their devotion.

Then one day, her penance of twice seven years was ended and Madeleine prepared again to leave the grotto. But this time, her heart was heavy at the thought of parting from the doe, the friendly beasts and the fowl of the air.

Now they gathered about her to bid her farewell. Blinded with tears, Madeleine embraced each animal. "Thank you, thank you, dear friends," she whispered, turned quickly and started for the slope. It was then the Voice rolled like music through the stillness.

"Madeleine, Holy Saint before the Lord, come to me in Paradise," the Voice commanded.

In that instant, the old legend says, Madeleine's face shone with a glory not of this world. "Wherever the Fairest One bids me come, there shall I go," she cried joyfully, for all at once she understood. The Holy Mother *had* kept her word!

Thereupon, according to many in Provence, Angels bore *la Sainte Madeleine* aloft on outstretched wings. Others claim that her purified soul took the form of a dove. "It ascended higher and higher, until it reached Paradise," they say. "Then the white dove flew straight through the Gates of Heaven."

How the Saint reached Paradise is neither here nor there. No one knows. But reach it she did. And to this day, as for hundreds of years, the young girls of Provence celebrate the event annually, on July 22, with *la Fête de la Madeleine*—the Festival of the Madeleine. With self-examination and prayer, they set out on a pilgrimage to the Holy Grotto at la Sainte Baume.

The girls plod up the steep rugged hillside to the chapel, now built on the reputed site of the grotto. There they kneel humbly, bow their heads and implore Saint Madeleine—who, at their age was so beautiful, sought after and had so many suitors—to help them find husbands —"and good ones, please," they add.

6 A CANDLE FOR ELIJAH
(Russia)

In the brave long-ago days when Saints walked the earth of Holy
Russia as men, young Danílo plowed, planted and raised rye on his
small patch of land. His grandfather, who left him his tidy little place
at the edge of the village, was a good farmer. And so was Danílo. His
rye was the best within miles, east or west.

Danílo was so industrious he seldom paused to pass the time of
day with Ivan, Vasily and the other lads in the village—or court the
girls, either. "When I don't have to make every minute count, I'll ask
Tamara to go dancing," Danílo promised himself, thinking how pretty
she looked in her new blouse with the embroidered sleeves. Yet for
the present, he was too busy with his rye to take time out for fun.

The only thing for which Danílo took time was to go to church,
burn a candle before the image of his favorite Saint, Nicholas, and ask
him to watch over his crops. "If I don't forget him, he'll not forget me,"
the youth confided to the village priest. "When I was a small lad, the
Saint watched over me, so my grandmother—*bábushka*—said. Now I'm
a man, he'll still protect me."

"You are right, my son," the old priest smiled with an approv-
ing nod. "Saint Nicholas protects the faithful."

This was true, though for long Danílo didn't know Saint Nicholas was protecting him from the Prophet Elijah—the quick-tempered
Saint with the fiery chariot, who liked to be first, when it came to

56

candles and prayers. If he thought a man was acting neglectful, like as not he'd rumble through the sky in his chariot and destroy his crops with storm and hail.

Early one day, Saint Nicholas and the Prophet, disguised as aged wanderers, were roaming the countryside. As was their wont, they stopped at this farm and that. If the owner was generous and kind, treated his beasts well and gave to the poor, he had naught to fear. But woe to the stingy, the slothful and greedy. Such farmers had cause to rue the Saints' displeasure!

When at last the pair reached Danílo's field, Nicholas' ruddy face creased in a smile. "Here's a pious peasant for you, Brother," he said, waving toward the rye, which glistened like gold in the late sun. "I'll see that he prospers in all he does. For hardworking and thrifty though the young fellow is, he never neglects to burn a candle in church in my honor—a ruble one, at that—come feast days."

When the Prophet, his brow black as thunder, rumbled jealously, "He doesn't, eh? I agree your peasant is thrifty—more thrifty than wise," Nicholas realized his mistake.

And moments later, when Elijah suddenly remembered urgent business elsewhere, took a hasty leave and swung down the road, Saint Nicholas was uneasy. "If I don't warn Danílo tonight, things may go hard with him, later," he reflected, turning over a scheme in his mind.

That evening when dusk had fallen, Nicholas knocked at Danílo's door. "Sst-tt! Have no fear, my son," said the Saint kindly, when he opened it, peered this way and that, and saw no one.

"W-who are you?" the youth faltered, trying to keep his voice steady. In spite of everything his spine prickled, his hands felt clammy cold.

But the next instant, when his visitor said, "I am Saint Nicholas, and your faithfulness pleases me," Danílo hugged himself in relief. "Listen carefully and all will be well," the voice from the shadows continued. "Hasten at once to the village priest and tell him you need money. Offer your field of standing rye for three hundred rubles."

Danílo gaped, swallowed hard and tried to thank the Saint. But when the youth realized he had gone, he lost no time in pulling on his boots, buttoning his jacket and bolting through the village. When his friend Vasily jeered, "Halloo-oo, what's the rush? Is your house afire?" Danílo pretended not to hear, and when long-legged Ivan tried to catch up, he ran faster. Even when the *Starósta*—Mayor—passed in his troika with the three high-stepping horses, the youth didn't stop to scrape and bow.

It wasn't till he'd raced by the onion-domed church at the far end of the village and knocked at the priest's door that Danílo paused for breath. And when the old man asked kindly, "Whatever's the matter, my son?" and motioned him to the stool near the fire, he was still panting.

"Nothing's the matter, Father, save my need for rubles," gasped Danílo, once he could speak. "I need rubles for seed, new thatch on the shed and a plowshare that will bite the earth. Tonight, when wondering what to do next, I remembered you said you had a nest egg— a small hoard you hoped one day to invest. Then I thought of my field. I'd sell it for three hundred rubles—if you cared to buy, that is. When harvest comes, in a short while, the *Starósta* would buy, I'm sure—at a tidy profit to you," he added eagerly.

The Priest stared at the fire, pulled at his sparse beard and rustled his shabby robe. "Three hundred rubles, eh?" he mumbled, thinking of the old sock under the mattress—the sock he'd scrimped to fill these thirty-odd years. It held the extra rubles for Christmas, the ruble at *Paskha*—Easter—kopecks from weddings, christenings and funerals. To increase his meager hoard had long been the old man's dream. Danílo's offer was a bargain, and yet—

"Three hundred rubles is a great sum—for the likes of a priest," the aged man found himself whining. But when he saw the youth's mind was made up and that no amount of haggling this way or that would change it, he shuffled off for the sock. And—lo!—after dumping its contents on the scrubbed pine table, stacking the tarnished silver and greenish coppers and counting them once, twice, thrice, he discovered he had exactly three hundred rubles—not a kopeck more nor a kopeck less. "Take them," he said hoarsely and pushed the pile toward Danílo. "I'll buy the field."

"And now you have a real nest egg, dear Father, I the money I need," cried Danílo, his eyes shining. Thanking the priest, he swept the coins into his pocket and bade him good night.

As Danílo raced home, the village was sleeping, the moon bright and round and his heart like a feather. "I've done as you commanded, dear Saint Nicholas," he said as he reached his door. "Though I don't know your reasons, I've sold the field."

But Danílo learned them, later. After days passed—neither too many nor yet too few—the priest's rye was lush and ripe and men were engaged to come with harvest hooks.

The night before, the Prophet Elijah rumbled through the skies in his fiery chariot. "I'll teach the young upstart a lesson," he muttered. "After tonight, he'll not forget to light a candle to the Saint with power to protect or ruin his grain."

So saying, the Prophet destroyed the rye. He beat it to the ground with wind and rain, severed it with hail and then scattered the golden grain heads like chaff.

Next morning, Elijah was in the field gloating over the destruction, when Nicholas approached. "Ho, Brother," the Prophet called gleefully, "as you see, I gave your pious peasant a lesson last night."

"Not the pious peasant, the pious Priest," corrected Nicholas, poking at the blasted grain with his toe. "The field is his."

Elijah's jaw dropped. "The Priest's, eh?" he exclaimed. "But I thought—I thought—"

"The field was Danílo's," finished Nicholas dryly. "So it was— until the Father invested his life savings in it."

"And now they're gone, and so is his rye," the Prophet rumbled contritely. "But I'll make amends. You'll see. I'll grow the field anew, make his rye twice as tall, double the crop. And as for your peasant," he added, "I'll see he gets the lesson he so dearly deserves."

That evening at dusk, Nicholas once more knocked on Danílo's door. "Go to the Priest and redeem your field," the Saint directed. "Buy it back with the three hundred rubles he paid." As before, he withdrew, and the youth lost no time in doing his bidding.

"I've come to make amends for your loss," Danílo told the Priest, moments later.

"Alas, no one can do that," moaned the Father, rocking back and forth before the fire. "What's gone is gone. I've lost my life savings, my rye is ruined and my field barren as the broad steppes to the east. Now naught save penury awaits my old age," he ended dismally, burying his face in his hands.

"That's where you're wrong, dear Father. You don't understand," cried the youth, plucking at the old man's sleeve. "That's why I'm here. I'm a farmer. I'll know what to do to make the field yield in time. *You* mustn't lose anything. I'm buying back the field for the exact same three hundred rubles you paid," he concluded, and the Father lifted his head and stared in astonishment.

When Danílo emptied his pockets, the Priest counted the rubles and stuffed them into the sock; he laughed and embraced the youth. "I always said you were pious, and now I know you are generous," the Father said.

Once more the days passed—neither too many nor too few—and the Prophet, still thinking the field was the Priest's, prospered it exceedingly. Elijah sent the little sun to warm the earth, the little rain to nourish the roots and gentle winds to strengthen the young new shoots that appeared as by magic.

And all the while, Danílo watched the rye and tended it lovingly. When finally the grain was full grown, and the heads heavy, he cut the rye. Then he bound the sheaves and stacked them in ricks, three and twenty to each. "Saint Nicholas has blessed me," he said. "Next week I'll thresh."

But before he did, the Saints again passed through the field. "See, Brother, how well I've done by the Father," the Prophet said, gazing with pride at the plump sheaves and high ricks. "When he threshes, I'll see the yield is greater than that of any man in these parts. To his dying day, the Priest will have reason to thank Saint Elijah."

Nicholas stifled a chuckle. "What you've done, Brother, is truly a wonder," he said. "But it's not the Priest, but the peasant, who'll thank Saint Elijah."

The Prophet blanched in anger. "*What?*" he roared. "What has the peasant to do with it?"

"Nothing—save he bought back the field, for the sum he paid, when you ravaged the Priest's property with hail," said Nicholas slyly.

The Prophet sputtered, swept the ricks of grain with baleful eye and then growled, "In that case, I'll take the good out of the youth's conniving. I'll see he gets no more than three measures of grain from each sheaf he drags to the threshing floor."

After Elijah strode away in a huff, without so much as a "Good day," Nicholas stroked his beard thoughtfully. "In that case, I'd best visit Danílo tonight," he chortled. "I'll instruct him to thresh sheaf by sheaf, instead of rick by rick. Then we'll see who gets the greatest yield of grain in these parts!"

Thus it was that Danílo, warned by his Patron, took his time about threshing. Each day, he threshed one sheaf—neither more nor less. Each day, his yield was abundant. He had more rye than he could sell, share with the Father or divide with the poor three parishes around. "Thank you, dear Saint Nicholas," the youth said each day. And when at last, all the sacks and bins in his barn overflowed, and he still had more grain to store than place to store it, he built a fine granary.

By the time the storehouse was finished, from stones on the floor to sods on the roof, Danílo had also finished threshing. And—lo!—the new granary burst with rye, as his heart with gratitude to his Patron.

Not long after, the Saints met in Danílo's courtyard. "Ho, what's the meaning of yonder storehouse?" demanded the Prophet testily. "Is your peasant improvident as he is conniving? With scarce enough grain to fill a dozen sacks, he has scant need of a granary."

"Oh, but you're mistaken, Brother," Nicholas said smiling. "His barn is full of grain, and so is his granary."

"Then tell me *how*," shouted Elijah, starting to check on his fingers. "What with but three measures of grain from each rick, and seven and thirty ricks, he'd—"

"Have no need for even a dozen sacks," his companion interrupted. "But you see, instead of ricks, he threshed by sheaves."

"Oh, ho, ho, I might have known, Brother," cried the Prophet, laughing in spite of himself. "Each time I chastise your pious peasant, you give everything away! But never mind," he added with a malicious grin, "I'll still remind him of my displeasure."

"What are you going to do?" asked Nicholas suspiciously.

"Oh, that I'll not say—this time," the Prophet replied, enjoying himself hugely.

Nicholas sighed. "Ah, well, if evil's intended, evil will be," he said in resignation. Then he bade his companion farewell and walked away, his head bowed.

It wasn't till evening that the Saint lifted his head, his brow clear and his laugh hearty. He'd thought of a plan—a plan so splendid it couldn't fail to soothe even the most ruffled feelings. "The best of Saints needs a bit of flattery, now and then," he declared and hurried to Danílo's door.

The following day Danílo, clutching two candles—one handsome, big and adorned with red roses and gilt leaves, the other a lean droopy dip with nothing on it—was rushing toward the onion-domed church at the end of the village. In his haste, he all but knocked down the two Saints—disguised as old bearded wayfarers—approaching from the opposite direction. "A hundred thousand pardons, kind Fathers," he exclaimed contritely. "In my haste to light candles to the Saints, I saw no one."

"The Saints, eh?" mumbled Elijah gruffly. "For which Saint, young man, do you intend that fine ruble candle?"

"Why, for Saint Elijah, of course," Danílo said quickly. "He's protected my rye and prospered the harvest—though before I bought my field back from the Priest, the Saint ravaged it with hail. But for me," he added, his face glowing, "he renewed the earth, grew rye with stouter stalks and longer heads. And as for the harvest—I needed a new granary for *that*!"

"The Saint will reward your gratitude," said the Prophet and then, pointing to the other candle, he asked abruptly, "For whom are you lighting the kopeck taper?"

"For Saint Nicholas," the youth said, dropping his voice. "You see, I'd not want him to feel hurt, or left out."

With an ill-concealed smirk, Elijah bade Danílo farewell and said, "God will bless you, my son."

As the two holy ones went about their business, Nicholas turned to the Prophet. "Well, there you are, Brother," he said, smiling in his beard. "You've seen for yourself how highly the peasant regards you, how little me—yet you accuse me of giving everything away to him," he added in a hurt voice.

"Tut, tut, you were right all along. I was wrong," replied the Prophet, more gratified than he cared to admit. "He is a pious youth, as you say. And he'll not suffer from devotion to the Saint with power to protect from hail."

And this Danílo never did. For from that day, until he died, many years later, he never forgot to show equal honor to both Saints. On the feast day of each, he burned candles of the exact same cost, length and girth—and painted with the exact same number of red roses and gilt leaves. And what's more, as time passed and he grew richer, his candles were bigger and cost more. When he knelt in church to chant a *Te Deum*, the youth always added a prayer, "Thank you, dear Saint Nicholas, for prospering my rye, and you, Saint Elijah, for sparing your hail."

But Saint Nicholas did more than prosper Danílo's rye. For now, what with things going so well, he had time to court the pretty Tamara. He took her dancing, skating and to fairs in the next village. And when, after a while she consented to wed him, he was the happiest young man for miles about. "Thank you, thank you, dear Saint," he said gratefully.

As the years came and went, Tamara and Danílo raised daughters and sons—as well as the finest rye anywhere. And as for the Priest—they looked after him. They saw to it his nest egg increased; he lacked for naught and spent a happy old age.

7 SAINT COLLEN AND THE SON OF NUDD

(Wales)

A long time ago, the folk of North Wales gave the name Llangollen —the Church of Collen—to a tiny settlement on the banks of the River Dee. "Collen was a hermit, a holy man who retired to a cave somewhere 'midst these green rolling hills," the inhabitants say proudly, gazing at their gorgeous countryside. But when you press for the exact proper spot of the cave—whether this side or the other of the River Dee, and whether among the high hills or low—they shake their heads. "No one knows," they admit. "But it must have been near. Else why did our forebears name this spot Llangollen? Why was the Church of Saint Collen founded, away back in the days when the Normans were Kings?"

Today Llangollen is a picturesque market town, the church still stands and the very old tell the strange tale of Saint Collen and the Son of Nudd.

Collen was a high churchman, an Abbot of Glastonbury, some say, before he decided he could serve the Lord better by taking his staff and going to Wales to spread the Word among the poor common folk there. That's how he came to wander the highways and byways of Wales and to preach to farmers and plowboys, tinkers with packs and cottagers, who wove woolen cloth for the rich folks in the towns.

But as time passed, Collen's locks turned gray, his beard snow white, and he grew more and more discouraged. He felt *he* somehow had failed. For no matter what he told these people of the glory and goodness of God, something—or *someone*—seemed to draw them into the ways of evil.

Yet who the someone was, the Saint didn't know. Sometimes, he'd come upon little knots of whisperers. He'd see the sly grins, hear mention of gold and then the name of one, Gwyn, Son of Nudd. Collen couldn't help wondering who Nudd was. Could there be some link 'twixt him and the Other-World King, Ned—or Old Nick—as some called him?

At last, baffled with failure, heavy with years and unable longer to wander, Saint Collen retired to a cave in a lush grassy hillside. With a rock for a door, a bubbling spring nearby and stillness all about, the holy man decided to end his days as a hermit. "In solitude and prayer I'll plead for my people," he said. "May God grant me grace to turn them from sins of envy and lust for gold."

Thus it came about that the aging Collen passed days and months in contemplation and prayer. And what with linnets and larks without the cave to add their praise to his, the spring to quench his thirst and trout from the stream, he lacked nothing needful. In the blessed solitude he grew in wisdom. His understanding of God's mysteries unfolded.

One morning early, when Collen as usual was kneeling at Matins, voices from without interrupted his devotions. Hard though he tried to remember his prayers, all was in vain. When at last the intruders mentioned the name of Gwyn, Son of Nudd, in considerable excitement, he rose from his knees, went to the mouth of the cave and strained his ears to catch each word. Standing there behind the rock, he could hear and yet not be seen.

On hearing the words "He's King of the Other-World," Collen frowned and pulled at his beard. So—his worst fears were confirmed. Nudd *was* the Evil One! When the Saint peered from the cave and saw the speakers—two Tiny Men no higher than his knee—his jaw dropped.

But when the taller of the Little Men said, "Ah, but that's not

all, Gwyn ab Nudd is also the King of the Fairies—the Fair Small
Folk," Saint Collen remembered he'd heard folks speak of them, too.

But now the Second Little Man was stammering, "Then—then
his kingdoms are two!" and Collen saw his small ruddy face blanch.

"That's what I'm telling you," said the First Small Man with a
wink. "That's why Gwyn is a good friend to have—if you want to get
on in this world and the next, as well."

By now Collen, unable to restrain his anger, thrust his head
from the cave and, "Hold your tongues!" he commanded, shaking his
fist at the Little Men. "Him of whom you speak is evil. And as for them
he rules—they are no better than Devils."

The Tiny Men turned and stared at the venerable hermit. Then
he who had spoken first laughed shrilly. "Hold our tongues, indeed!" he
said, adding rudely, "Hold your own tongue, old man—unless it's a
rebuke you're after."

"That we shall see," replied Collen, and, returning to his Matins, sought to free his mind of the matter.

But early next day, Collen's devotions again were disturbed,
this time by a loud pounding at the entrance to the cave. At first he
paid no heed, but when the knocks continued and a voice demanded
sharply, "Hermit Collen, are you within?" there was nothing to do but
reply.

"Aye, that I am," Collen said. "Who wants me?"

"A messenger from His Majesty, Gwyn ab Nudd, King of the
Other-World and of the Fair Small Folk," the voice answered. "He
would have speech with you. He commands you to meet him tomorrow, at high noon precisely, on the brow of the hill."

"That we shall see," replied Collen by way of refusal and returned to his meditations. Before he met with this Son of Nudd, he
must have more time to think, pray and learn God's will.

The next day came and went, and with it the noonday hour.
But Collen paid no heed to the King's summons.

The following day, however, again brought the loud knocking.
As before, the King's envoy shouted, "Hermit Collen, are you within?"

"Yea, yea, I am," replied Collen testily. "What do you want
with me?"

"You are summoned a second time to the presence of King Gwyn ab Nudd. He bids you to meet him without fail tomorrow, on top of the hill."

This time Collen deigned no reply but returned to his prayers. He was not yet ready to meet Gwyn ab Nudd.

But after the appointed hour and the appointed day passed once again, and the Saint neither stuck his head from his cell nor put in an appearance, he wasn't surprised when for the third time, angry knocks disturbed his peace. Nor was he surprised when the messenger asked harshly, Was he within? delivered the same command, and added a threat, "This time, old man, you'd best heed the summons of your own accord, come to the hill and present yourself to His Majesty. Otherwise, things may be the worse for you."

God has a time for everything, Collen mused, smiling in his beard. The time had come and he was ready to obey the summons. "Tell your Master to expect me," he said briefly and busied himself with preparations for the forthcoming meeting.

The next day, Collen rose calm in mind, strong in spirit and eager to meet his adversary. Well before noon he filled a flask with holy water, tucked the bottle inside his belt and knelt for guidance. "With this blessed water, God's help—and a bit of luck—I can rout all the Demons in Hell," he said with confidence, when he rose. Then he reached for his staff, left the cave and started the long ascent to the knoll.

Never was sun brighter, sky more blue, or did the larks pour forth such sweet song. Yet to Collen the way seemed steeper, his limbs stiffer—and he had to rest more often for breath—than ever before. Still, as he approached the crest of the hill, his spirit was yet stronger, his heart pounded with excitement and his eyes sparkled.

It was close to noon when Collen paused to rest for the last time. Leaning on his staff, he took a deep breath and glanced up, to see how far he must go. Then he gasped in astonishment. On the top of the knoll—where before nothing had ever been save green grass and gray rock—arose a gleaming castle, complete with turrets and towers. Silken standards—burning red in color and worked in blue, cold as ice—whipped from the battlements. "The colors of Satan," murmured the Saint and touched the bottle.

But what surprised Collen most about the splendid scene was its size. Only a man no taller than a toddler could enter that castle, walk in those gardens or stroll 'neath the trees, laden with rare fruits and exotic flowers. As he drew nearer, he saw fair-haired maidens in rainbow robes floating down flower-bordered paths, hand in hand with handsome youths. Both maidens and youths were tiny—and so were the black spirited horses he saw in the distance. On their backs they bore knights in silver armor, with plumes on their helmets and spurs on their heels.

Gazing at the lively scene, Collen paused and pulled at his beard. Then all at once, recalling the words of the Tiny Men outside his cell, he exclaimed, "Ah-h, to be sure. These are the ones they called Fairies—the Small Fair Folk Gwyn rules!"

Thereupon, Collen stood without the castle gates, handwrought of gold and set with sapphires and rubies. He heard music and saw minstrels picking at strings of harp, piping on flutes and beating drums. Now the maidens danced and gazed into the eyes of the bearded youths.

Yet Collen, peering through the gates, still was perplexed. How could he, a mortal, pass through them, enter the castle and keep tryst with the King? Just as the Saint was wondering what to do next, his fingers once more touched the bottle of holy water. Then the miracle happened!

Now whether Collen grew smaller or the Fair Small Folk, the castle and everything in it grew bigger, he didn't know—either then, or later, when in solitude he pondered the power of the holy water. All he knew was that the gates flew open instantly, he walked through, and squires, attired in the red and blue of their Master, sprang forward to welcome him, bow at his feet and escort him to the castle door.

There a man with snow-white hair and flowing robe stepped forward and greeted Collen with quiet dignity. "In the name of my Master, the King, I bid you welcome," the venerable man said. "Pray follow me. I shall take you to His Majesty, who awaits you in the royal dining hall."

"So—he thinks to deceive me with meat, drink and gracious words," thought Collen, as his guide swept before him through dimly lit corridors, supported by columns of fluted gold. From the walls hung rare tapestries, and from the ceilings golden lamps, encrusted with gems of blue and red. In the faint light, they blinked and glimmered as brightly as stars in the sky. But there was no time to admire these wonders, for already the white-haired one stood before a closed door. The next instant, he threw it open and presented the Saint to Gwyn, Son of Nudd—a personage of regal bearing, flashing eye and in appearance, neither old nor young.

"My greetings to you, Hermit Collen," said the monarch. "And with our own, greetings from my two kingdoms—the Other-World and that of the Fair Small Folk."

His eyes on the face of the King, Collen replied sternly, "And to you the greeting that you and your kingdoms merit."

Gwyn's eyes narrowed speculatively. Then he motioned to a golden table set with all manner of dainties intended to tempt the palate and delight the eye. "Pray be seated," he said blandly, indicating a golden chair. "You shall eat and drink with me. And should you desire aught that is not here, you have but to ask," he added hospitably. "Your wish expressed is fulfilled."

Thereupon, servants liveried in red and blue stepped forward to seat the King and his guest. "Come, eat and drink with me. Let us talk," Gwyn urged. For when the servants poured out ruby wine and offered rich foods from golden platters, he saw that Collen touched nothing.

"Nay, Gwyn, Son of Nudd," cried Collen, his eyes blazing. "With such as you, I shall neither eat fruit from your vine nor sip dew from your grass."

"And why not?" the King demanded, blanching in anger. "Have you yet seen castle more splendid, finer foods or servitors better equipped than these of mine?"

"For such as these things are, 'tis well enough," replied the Saint scornfully. "Yet, not for all I hold holy, would I don the colors this castle flies, and these men wear."

Though the King's dark eyes smoldered like embers, his voice was smooth as silk. "Explain your meaning, Hermit Collen," he said, feigning ignorance.

"That I shall, Gwyn, son of Nudd—though already my meaning must be clear," thundered Collen, half rising. "The red your minions wear signifies the burning fires of Hell; ice-blue, the cruel heart of the Other-World King."

Even as Gwyn reached for the dagger at his side, Collen whipped the bottle from his belt. Then he sprinkled the holy water over the head of the King, those of his servants and about the four corners. "Begone, Son of Darkness—you and these Devils who serve you, disguised as the Fair Folk," the Saint commanded and sprinkled more water. "Never return to this land to dazzle men's eyes with gold, turn their hearts from God, or tempt them with your tawdry splendors."

The words had scarcely left Saint Collen's lips when—lo!— Gwyn ab Nudd vanished, together with his servitors. And so did the minstrels, the ladies and youths—and even the fine castle and gardens.

All vanished in a trice, according to the old legend. And there on the crest of the hill stood Saint Collen alone, with the noonday sun shining like a halo around his head. "God works in mysterious ways," he said, glancing first at the empty flask, then across the green grass and gray rocks. And forthwith, offering praise for the miracle, he grasped his staff, descended the hill and returned to his cave.

"From that day, until the Lord took his soul to Heaven, Saint Collen never again saw the Son of Nudd or the Small Folk," the people of Llangollen declare. "Nor have we!" they add, and end by saying:

> The old graybeard still tells this tale
> As his father said
> *His* father's father told it to him.
> 'Tis the selfsame story I'm repeating now,
> In the selfsame way.

8 THE MAN WITH THE SHREWISH WIFE

(Ireland)

To this day, the old folk of Ireland have a strange expression, "As far as Tig-na-Vauria from Donaghadee." And when you inquire what it means, they chuckle—as over a secret joke—and crinkle their leathery faces in a grin. "Wisha, an' have you never heard of Saint Brandon and the man with the shrewish wife?" they ask.

And when you shake your head, they laugh outright, the old ones do, stuff their clay dudeens—pipes—and proceed with the tale that generations of parents have told generations of the young—goodness knows for how many years.

But 'twas long ago that the woodcutter, Donagha Dee, and his wife, Vauria, lived in County Kerry, in a mean hut at the edge of the forest. In those days, mind you, Ireland was different. There were more trees, where settlements and farms are today. Why, in those times, folks claimed a nimble squirrel could travel all the way from Kerry to Cork, and not so much as touch foot to ground!

Of course, that's neither here nor there so far as our tale is concerned, save that a poor man was free to cut all the wood he wanted to burn for himself or sell to the rich folk roundabout.

Donagha, who worked harder, and was poorer, than most, always seemed to have less to show for his pains than other men—or so Vauria kept reminding him.

73

From dawn to dark, he chopped trees, cut them neatly and lugged the wood to the village to sell. Yet for all his industry, it was hard to eke out a living for the two. For what with wood plenty, money scarce and both lord o' the manor and the squire on the hill penny pinchers, he seldom had enough sixpences and shillings to satisfy his shrewish wife.

"So—and you expect me to fill your stomach with mush and potatoes on *that!*" Vauria would scold, tossing down the scant earnings in disgust. "Why I married such a good-for-nothing stocagh I'll never know!"

Nor did Donagha know why he'd married a woman who was a shrew and had a tongue like a whip—though he had the grace not to say so. "I've made my bed and I'll lie in it," he told himself resolutely, and bit back angry words, though Vauria saw to it he got no peace. Even when he'd slogged home bone-tired, and his back breaking under his load, she was after him. The minute he lighted his dudeen and sat down for a quiet smoke, she belabored him for tracking in mud—after she'd scrubbed fingers to the bone, trying to clean up the hovel. Then she'd order him to poke up the fire or fetch the water for tea.

Now to bear the cross of a nagging wife is hard on a man, even if she has a pretty face or a heart of gold. But Vauria, alas—who used to have both—had lost them long since. And what with the frown on her brow, the discontent in her eyes and the corners of her mouth pulled down, Donagha was often of a mind to think her ugly as the Old Gentleman himself. "But if I hold my tongue, she may change one day," the woodcutter told himself hopefully, "and return mayhap to the sweet colleen I once knew."

Yet after a while, even Donagha had to admit Vauria never changed—save for the worse. 'Twas truly a dog-and-cattish life the pair led. And as time dragged by and her tongue grew more waspish, he was that bothered he took to wondering how much longer he could stand the nagging. Then along came that beautiful fine day in May that brought about an unexpected turn in the lives of the two.

That day Vauria slipped from bed early. And to spite Donagha

—that weary he was still snoring like a trooper—she rattled pans and dropped pots till he sat up with a start. "Sure, and what's the matter?" he mumbled stupidly.

"Matter indeed! As if you weren't the laziest lout in three parishes, Donagha Dee," shrilled Vauria, spoiling for a fight. "Things have reached a pretty pass when I, your wife, build the fire and fetch the water so his lordship can sleep." So saying, she snatched up a firkin, and flounced to the well.

That was the end of sleep for Donagha. Though still too early to rise, he sighed, climbed from bed and pulled on his clothes. The next moment, touching the dudeen in his pocket, he grinned sheepishly. With luck, he'd be able to get a puff or two, before Vauria returned.

But luck wasn't with Donagha. When Vauria returned to find him in the chimney corner and waiting for his tea, a thousand beagles barked from her throat. "Well, so it's that way," she screamed, slopping water. "Have you naught this blessed day to do, but sit by the fire like a fine gentleman, dudeen in jaw, while I wait on you?"

When Donagha puffed smoke rings and made no reply, Vauria's rage flared even more. After letting out a torrent of words I'd not dare repeat, she ended, "Faith, and might it not be more fitting, if you went to the forest and fetched home a brosna—firewood—than to sit there, as though a twelvepenny nail held the seat o' your breeches to the seat o' the bench?"

By this time Donagha, who couldn't hold his tongue longer, decided a good retreat was better than a bad fight. Consequently, he quickly gathered up his ax, billhook and rope and made for the forest, without so much as a word.

But once out of sight of Vauria's pulled-down mouth and out of hearing of her ugly words, 'twas as though Donagha were born again. The weight of the world slipped from his shoulders. For the first time, he felt the fine beautiful day, the sun on his neck and heard little birds piping merrily. He smelled the sweetness of windflower and violet. Oh, such a fine day it was, it gave the heart a lilt, joy to being young and alive and forgetfulness to mean horrid words. By the time he reached the middle of the forest and set to work with his ax, he was humming softly. Soon his whistle was lusty, as though there were nothing at all to fret him.

Now whether he was wool-gathering or whether he wasn't—what with the day and the gladness about him—Donagha couldn't remember, later, when he tried to piece things together. But when the Voice from somewhere behind spoke his name, he jumped. He was that frightened and surprised he let the blade of the ax nick his thumb.

"Donagha Dee, Donagha Dee," the Voice repeated, softer and sweeter than the voice of the birds. "Don't be afraid."

Donagha swung around quickly. But seeing no one, he couldn't help being more frightened than before. "Where are you, and *w-who* are you?" he faltered, peering behind the trees and through the low-hanging branches. But still when he saw no one, his knees knocked in terror.

Only then did Donagha notice the rippling of leaves in a certain bush. When he heard something like laughter, and then the Voice spoke from the leaves, fear left him. "For sure, lad, I'm only Saint Brandon, sent to give you a message," it said. "It's two wishes you're being given—for being a Christian, what with holding your tongue and bearing the cross of a shrewish wife."

"Two wishes!" exclaimed Donagha, his heart pounding. "Troth, and what couldn't a man do with wishes!" He was just thinking of what his old granddad told him as a boy, "If wishes were gold pieces, lad, we'd all ride in coaches." But the Voice was speaking again.

"Mind this, Donagha Dee," the Saint warned. "Think well before you wish. A wish once spoken is gone forever."

"Och, and I'll mind it, good Saint Brandon," cried Donagha, his eyes shining. "And it's grateful I am to you for such a fine gift."

The leaves rustled gently. And the next moment, knowing the Saint had left, Donagha picked up his ax and returned to chopping. All the while he was cutting the neatest pile of firewood a body ever saw, he was thinking what he should wish. His thoughts flew faster than his

hands, as he turned over this and that in his mind. Should he choose first off, riches, a good wife—better still, no wife at all? He was that occupied with the first wish he never got to the second that day!

By nightfall, though his brosna was chopped and tied securely with the rope, Donagha still hadn't decided what to wish for. It wasn't till he heaved the bundle to his back, staggered ahead a few yards— and then stumbled with weariness—that he saw how foolish he'd been. "I was that occupied with wishes, I chopped more wood than three donkeys could carry," he grumbled, stopping short. Then he eased down his burden, wiped his brow and took a deep breath.

Tuckered as he was, and with no place to sit save the ground, Donagha straddled the brosna to rest, glance about at the deepening twilight and try to decide what to do next. If he left the wood where it was and returned, the next day, to fetch it, Vauria would never let him hear the end of his laziness. On the other hand, even if he had strength to lug the heavy thing home tonight, he'd be late—so late he'd get a dressing down he couldn't take, being so fagged and all. "Either way, you're in a fix, Donagha Dee," he exclaimed, exasperated beyond endurance. "I wish to Heaven this silly brosna could carry *me*, instead of my carrying it!"

Well, no sooner were the words out of his mouth than poor Donagha knew what he'd done. He'd wasted one of his two precious wishes, and no power on earth could recall it. The wood under him shuddered and shook. Before he knew it, it reared like a living beast, tottered an instant and then raced away at a hair-raising gallop. Holding on for dear life, he blamed himself as a fool and yelled a thousand murders. But that's all the good it did. The brosna raced on. Like a colt with kicking heels, it darted between trees, hopped over humpy roots and leaped across boulders and rocks.

It was that nerve-shattering to Donagha he was still yelling when the wood shot through the gate, halted at the shed and then collapsed, hurling him to the ground with a bone-shaking thud. And there, at the door stood Vauria, seeing it all, ready to lambaste him, and say that thanks to him, supper was spoiled. But wonders of wonders! For once she was speechless. As he limped toward her, it was easy to see she was shaken. Her jaw had dropped and she was gaping from seeing her husband so strangely mounted.

But not for long, mind you. When Donagha tried to enter the house, Vauria's power of speech returned. "No, you don't—not till you tell me what's going on," she shrilled and blocked his way. "You don't go a step farther till you say what that—that *thing* is, and what you've been doing all day."

It didn't help matters when Donagha said gruffly, "Chopping wood—and even you should know a brosna when you see one!" and brushed past Vauria. Nor was her temper improved when he fumbled for his dudeen, lighted it and started to puff without saying more.

"So—you were chopping wood, eh?" screamed Vauria, her eyes like gimlets. And I suppose you didn't meet up with a Devil or Witch, who enchanted the wood and packed you home yelling at the top o' your lungs! If you don't say whom you met and what happened, Donagha Dee, you'll live to regret it," she ended threateningly.

Donagha took a puff or two before he replied. "I met a Saint— Saint Brandon hisself," said he reluctantly, for he had no wish to tell *all* that had happened in the forest. Still, with those boring eyes on his face, he had to say something.

"Oho, *you* met a Saint—a likely tale, that!" sneered Vauria meanly. "And pray, what would a Saint want with the likes o' you?"

"He gave me two wishes," Donagha said and then, because he saw no way out of telling the rest of the story, he confessed how that night, coming home, he'd wasted one of them. "When I sat down to rest, I was that weary I couldn't drag one foot after the other. That's when I forgot, and wished the brosna would carry me home," he ended, hanging his head and added quickly, "But I still have another."

Vauria's eyes glittered with greed. "Give it to me and *I'll* know what to wish for," she wheedled craftily.

But when Donagha shook his head and reminded her, " 'Twas Saint Brandon as gave the wishes to *me*," Vauria turned on him in fury.

"You—you—idiot, puddinghead, fool!" shouted the angry woman. "If you hadn't been too lazy to walk home like other wood-cutters, I could be rich now. Instead of scrubbing and scrimping and wearing rags, I'd be a fine lady, with satin on my back, jewels on my fingers and my feet in slippers with heels. But no, you had to throw away my luck. You didn't think of me, your wife, who gave you her best years, cooks your stew, mends your clothes and—and—" Overcome by self-pity, she sat down and blubbered till the rafters shook.

"And makes his life miserable with her shrewish nagging," roared Donagha, jumping to his feet and shaking his fist—for all at once the patience inside him snapped. Then he grinned. "I wish to Heaven the whole of Erin might lie 'twixt you and me!" he added deliberately.

"And—wisha!—that's what happened," say those who tell this tale. "Quicker than the poor henpecked man could flick an eyelash, a whirlwind whipped him up, whisked him away and landed him on the most northeastern tip of Ireland. And there, off the North Channel, in a hamlet called Donaghadee to this day, he lived in comfort and peace, with Saint Brandon to watch over him.

"And as for his wife," your informants continue, "the same stiff whirlwind took care of *her*—and good riddance it was. For it whistled her westward, toward the Atlantic, beyond Dingle, on Dingle Bay. Though no one has ever heard, or taken pains to find out, what she did without Donagha to scold, people named the place she lived, Tig-na-Vauria, or 'Vauria's House.'

"So there you have it," the old ones conclude. "Now you know why we Irish say, 'As far as Tig-na-Vauria from Donaghadee,' when we mean two persons are as far apart as east is from west."

9 THE SAINT WHO TWEAKED SATAN'S NOSE

(England)

According to English legend, the harrowing events I'm about to describe occurred more than a thousand years ago, at Glastonbury Abbey—when Saint Dunstan was a monk and the Devil decided to take his soul.

Even before he became a monk, Satan hated Saint Dunstan. For aside from the fact that everyone—from the King on his throne to the pauper on the street—loved him, his reputation for piety was great. People said he'd had heavenly visions, strange dreams and even performed miracles. But strangest of all was his singing. When he played his harp and sang anthems—which he did with exceeding sweetness—his listeners sank in awe to their knees. "The Angels taught him the words!" they said. Then they predicted, "He'll give himself to God—and be the next Archbishop of Canterbury."

As if rumors such as these weren't enough to upset the Devil, there was Saint Dunstan's generosity. He was greedy for his poor—greedier than most men for themselves. Though wealthy to start, after he'd given all he had to the needy, he borrowed, begged and skimped on himself, to get more. "*He* goes threadbare, in order to clothe his beggars," the Saint's family complained.

In addition to all else, Saint Dunstan's hobby of metalwork irked Satan. The young man's skill endeared him to every craftsman in the land. "He was born to the hammer," they boasted, and regarded him as a son. For what with a forge and anvil, metal of any sort and a hammer, there wasn't anything he couldn't make—from a fine gold cup, embossed with flowers and fruits, to a silver brooch or an iron shoe for a beast.

Altogether, Satan was uneasy about the young man—more so than he cared to admit. And once Saint Dunstan renounced the world, shaved his head and entered the monastery as a monk, the Devil schemed night and day for his soul. "If I don't seize the wretched thing, drag it away and burn it in fire—before he's Archbishop—he'll bag more souls for Heaven than I for Hell," the Evil One muttered glumly.

It was this nagging worry about tripping the Saint—and not knowing how—that prompted Satan to use his magic power of making himself invisible. "That way," he plotted, one day, "I can follow the fellow everywhere, snoop in corners and listen at keyholes—with no one the wiser. I'll learn how to catch him—in time," he ended with a leer.

A short time later, when the Abbot was talking to Saint Dunstan, and Satan, as usual, was skulking unseen in the shadows, he thought his long-awaited opportunity had come.

The Abbot had just proposed to the young monk that he build an anvil and forge, make a smithy of his cell and continue, in spare time, his hobby of metalcraft. "You have need of your hammer, my son, we of your skill," the old man said kindly. "Our Lord has blessed your hands, as well as your mind, and given them power to make sacred ornaments. Only they can fashion a golden chalice, worthy of this Holy House."

"Thank you, dear Father," cried Saint Dunstan, face shining. "I've missed my hammer since becoming a monk. I fear I sing praises better standing at the anvil, hammer in hand, than from my knees," he confessed and went on happily, "Besides the chalice, I'll create a pyx for the Host, a silver crucifix that will make men seek repentance and—"

The Abbot held up a hand. "Never fear, my son, we shall keep you busy," he interrupted, smiling. "Satan finds work for idle hands!"

And busy ones, ha, ha! thought Satan from the shadows. For the old man's words had given him an idea—an idea so splendid it had to succeed! *Now I know how to fix him,* he sneered, a wicked smile twisting his lips. *The silly fool will give away anything—even his Soul—for his poor.*

The Devil waited impatiently for the smithy to be finished. Then one evening toward dusk, when Saint Dunstan's deep voice floated across the fields in praise to the lusty accompaniment of hammerblows, Satan knew the stage was set for his scheme. "It's time to pay a call on the pie-faced priest," he shouted and pried the iron shoe from one cloven hoof.

Then the Devil dressed in his best black tights, draped his long tail nattily over his arm, like a walking stick, and loped toward the abbey in the deepening dusk.

On reaching the Saint's cell, the Devil peered inside. And when he saw the holy man bending at the forge, back toward him, Satan poked his horned head through the window, cleared his throat and rasped, "Hem—good evening, Saint."

Saint Dunstan spun around quickly. And on finding himself staring into the dark wicked face—seeing the pricked-up horns, the leer on the lips and the bright bulgy eyes—his spine tingled and his knees knocked in terror. Yet, "What brings you here, Devil?" he demanded sternly, struggling to keep his voice steady.

"My need for a shoe—which you alone have the skill to fit to the rim of a cloven hoof." Satan smirked. "When I caught my hoof in a crevice, wrenched free, but found I'd left my shoe behind in a crack, I thought of you," he lied glibly and added slyly, "Folks say you're kind and never turn anyone—even sinners—away without help."

"And what makes you think I'd help *you?*" thundered Saint Dunstan.

"Because I'll pay in gold—as much gold as you want for your poor," chortled Satan and added, eyes glittering and horns trembling in excitement, "If you love them as much as you say, you'll give up *something,* to feed every beggar in Britain, clothe him like a prince and give him a fine house to live in. Besides, you'd be the saintliest Saint in the world!" he ended with a leer.

"Mmm—mmm—gold for my poor," mumbled the Saint, who pretended to consider the offer, while gaining time to decide what to do. "And in return for the gold, you want me to give up—"

"Your soul! How clever to guess!" the Devil shouted. "But don't worry. I'd not collect payment till you've had your fun, seen your paupers strut like lords and are too old, anyway, to care about Heaven. I'd not come till then. Then I'd heave your worthless soul to my back, tote it, like a sack of meal, to Hell and fry it to a crisp! A fine bargain, eh, Saint?" he ended, his eyes glowing like the embers on the hearth.

"Aye, a fine bargain—for my poor," groaned the holy man, still pretending to turn over the dreadful bargain in his mind. But now he was considering a daring scheme—a scheme to outwit the Devil, drive him away and save his, Dunstan's, soul.

But when the Saint didn't speak at once, Satan grated threateningly. "*Well?* Do I have to wait all night for you to decide?"

Still saying nothing, Saint Dunstan—to hide the crafty smile on his lips—poked at the fire. Then, sighing deeply, he turned to the door, opened it and said shortly, "Come in, Devil. I'll shoe you—for the sake of my poor."

"Aha, Saint, I thought you'd see things *my* way," chuckled Satan and leaped like a grasshopper through the door.

The Devil watched sharply as the Saint—with the air of one who wants to get on with a bad business—tied a leather apron over his robe, bustled from forge to anvil and prepared to make the shoe. He set aside the gold cup he'd been making, put iron on the anvil and hauled from a corner blacksmith tools—pincers, pliers and the thin long-handled tongs that looked like giant scissors.

Then the Saint set to work. With a few deft strokes he hammered the iron into a shoe. Then he made nails—long and needle-sharp at the end. But his hands flew so swiftly Satan didn't see their sharpness or length. All he saw were the sparks that crackled, snapped and darted about the cell. "Ha, ha, now you're working for *me*, Saint!" he

taunted, hopping about gleefully. "I can see you'll be useful when I get you to Hell."

"Hmm, we'll see what we'll see," said the holy man dryly. Then he stoked the fire, blew with the bellows and thrust the tongs—and also the nails—to heat in the forge. "A blacksmith's cold tongs are worse than a carpenter's dull saw," he explained, eyes innocent and wide.

By now Satan, pleased at the way things were going—and his own cleverness—was in rare good humor. Even when the Saint briskly tied one end of a rope to a peg on the wall, made a loop with a slip-knot in the other end, and said smoothly, "Rest your foot in the loop, while I try the shoe," the Devil's suspicions weren't aroused.

With Satan's foot in the loop, the Saint tried on the shoe, ran a finger around the rim of the hoof and said in a pleased voice, "As fine a fit as you'd see—if I say so myself—though it's the first time I've made an iron shoe for a cloven hoof."

"But it won't be the last!" jeered Satan, ordered the Saint to stop mooning and get on with the shoeing.

And this the good man did with all speed, and the Devil realized, too late, his dreadful mistake.

For now the Saint reached for pincers, nipped a glowing nail from the forge, and then, with one awful hammerblow, sent the searing needle-sharp point through shoe, hoof, and deep into the Evil One's flesh.

"*Ouch!* O-U-C-H! Satan shrieked, blanching. "Scoundrel—rascal—swindling monk—" He reached dark bony fingers toward the Saint, tore at the rope that held his ankle in a hangman's noose and uttered dreadful words I'd not dare repeat. But the more the Devil thrashed, the harder he yanked, and the more desperately he tried to pull away from the wall, the closer the loop slipped and the more searing the pain. "Let me go-oo-ooo," he blubbered wildly and squirmed, like a worm on a hook.

"Not till I've finished nailing your shoe," said the holy man grimly, a malicious glint in his eyes. "That's what you wanted, and that's what you'll get," he added and nipped a second nail from the forge.

"No, no," screamed Satan. And now his eyes—round and glassy as marbles—all but popped from his head.

What happened next, I'll not describe. The scene was too harrowing. Suffice it to say, the doughty Saint managed—goodness knows how—to drive the second glowing nail through Satan's hoof and into his foot. But when Saint Dunstan tried to drive the third nail in, Satan broke loose and lunged toward the door and all but escaped.

But Saint Dunstan was quicker than he. "No you don't—not till I'm done with you," the good man thundered, whipped the long-handled blacksmith tongs from the fire and clamped the Evil One's thin nose in the red-hot tips. Then he gave a horrible tweak.

"Oh, my n-nose! My N-O-S-E!" shrilled Satan, collapsed on the floor and lay in a heap like a dirty dark rag. "Let my nose a-alone," he moaned, shuddering, "and I'll g-go—"

"*Where?*" the Saint roared, and gave another tweak with the tongs.

"Back to H-Hell," whimpered the Devil.

"Then go—and good riddance," Saint Dunstan bawled. "And if you dare show your prying nose hereabouts again, you'll get worse." And so saying, he dragged the screeching Demon to the door and flung him into the darkness. Then he re-entered his cell, shoulders shaking with laughter.

When at length Satan recovered sufficiently to stagger to his feet, he limped away as fast as he could through the streets of Glastonbury —what with nails in his foot and nose burning. As he stumbled over the cobblestones, his horns drooped like wilted weeds, his tail dragged in the dust and shoulders sagged. "Oh, what has the baldhead done to me? What has he done?" he howled.

The Devil's lamentations were so fearsome and loud that honest folk, asleep in their beds, roused with a start, rushed to windows and peered through the shutters. And when they beheld the Devil—toiling through the street screaming with pain—they laughed at his wretched plight. Like Saint Dunstan, they yelled, "Good riddance!"

But now Satan roared even louder—so loudly, in fact, that folk, three leagues distant, heard his bellowings plainly. Some, living at least

seven leagues from Glastonbury, claimed they, also, heard the earsplit-
ting shrieks and wails. Now whether they were right or whether they
weren't, we don't know—after more than a thousand years. All we
know is, that writing of the event, Mother Goose—who *always* was
right—said the awful din was heard *"nine* leagues and more!" across
the countryside.

> Saint Dunstan, as the story goes,
> Once pulled the Devil by the nose
> With red-hot tongs—which made him roar
> That he was heard nine leagues and more.

And as for Saint Dunstan, after his dreadful tussle with Satan,
he grew in wisdom and grace, became a priest and then—as everyone
predicted—the next Archbishop of Canterbury. He was also a great
statesman, Britain's first Prime Minister and, most important of all,
Patron of schoolboys.

"Sweet Father Dunstan," they called him, for the holy man was
their friend. "If we invoke his name—and have done no wrong—he will
protect us," the boys said.

And so it seemed. For if a Master accused a lad unjustly,
ordered him to bend over and raised a cane to flog him, one of two
things happened. Either the Master, overcome by strange drowsiness,
would fall asleep instantly or else the cane would clatter from his hand
to the floor. Either way, thanks to their Patron Saint, innocent boys
escaped unharmed!

But besides protecting schoolboys, Sweet Father Dunstan entertained them. Even when an old man, at Canterbury, the head of the
church and adviser to kings, his greatest delight was to gather his
"sons" for a story hour beside his hearth. Looking into their eager
faces, he'd smile benignly and ask, "What story shall I tell tonight?"

The answer was always the same. "Dear Father Dunstan," the
lads clamored, "tell us how you tweaked Satan's nose, drove him back
to Hell and saved your soul—when you were a monk at Glastonbury."

10 THE PENANCE OF FILIPPO PIPETTA
(Italy)

Filippo Pipetta was a university student in Rome when his great-uncle died, leaving the young man a musty old book bound in sheepskin. The moment Filippo opened the book, riffled through the yellowed pages and saw the strange symbols and spells his uncle had written in his tall spidery hand, the youth whooped with delight. "Oho, so the old man wasn't so solemn as we all supposed!" he cried, as he tried out a spell or two. From that moment he forsook the study of the stars and took up all kinds of sorcery.

And small wonder. For when Filippo discovered the marvelous things he could do by mumbling a few magic words—or just clapping his hands back to back—he could think of nothing else. He changed quickly from an industrious student, who gave promise of being a great astronomer, to an idle fun-loving fellow, whom his friends loved and the authorities feared.

Now there was no end to Filippo's pranks. Whether the city fathers clapped him in jail for practicing witchcraft or whether they didn't, mattered little. He always escaped and made fools of his keepers.

Once, his jailors put Filippo into a cell, locked the door and even saw him asleep. But in the morning their prisoner was gone! And to make matters worse, on the pillow where the night before they'd seen his head, lay the head of a donkey!

Even more mortifying was the night some weeks later, when the authorities arrested Filippo and six merry companions for disturbing the sleep of honest folk. That time, the guards not only locked, but bolted, the cell door. "Good night, and no tricks, mind you," they growled. "We'll be just outside—in case you get notions."

Filippo grinned and said nothing. But no sooner had the key turned and the bolt squeaked into place than he winked to his friends and whipped out a bit of charcoal. With a few deft strokes on the cell wall, he drew a boat, mumbled a spell and beckoned his companions to follow him.

No one knew exactly what happened next. But come morning, the jailors found the cell empty, saw the picture and heard rumors that made them red in the face. At least a dozen reliable citizens reported they'd seen seven stalwart young men rowing up the Tiber at daybreak!

"He mocks the law and makes fools of us all," the judges complained, after each escapade. The most learned lawyers in Rome were powerless against Filippo's tricks.

But escaping from cells wasn't *all* that Filippo had mastered. That was the fun of magic. When he wanted anything—gold in his purse, wine on the table or clothes on his back—all he had to do was clap his hands back to back, and murmur a word or two. Instantly three young Devils with dark grinning faces, wings on their shoulders and stubby horns on their heads appeared, asking, "What does the Master want?"

No sooner would Filippo express a wish than the Devils fulfilled it. Yet for all his mischievous tricks, baffling disappearances and poking fun at his betters, Filippo wasn't stingy or mean. More often than not, when he demanded wealth from a Devil, it wasn't for himself. Like as not, he'd share with the needy, help some threadbare student or drop into the alms box at church a piece of gold—and watch the priest's face when he found it.

It was a merry life—so long as it lasted. Then one dreadful day, Filippo met the Man in Black.

That day, Filippo was hurrying through the square on an

errand. He'd just passed the time of day with the old flower woman, dropped a coin in her lap and had reached the stone steps of the church when he felt the urge to glance over his shoulder. When he saw the Man in Black following at a distance, the blood froze in his veins.

Filippo Pipetta didn't have to be told that the Man with the thin cruel lips, eyes that flickered and flared and the long black cloak was Satan, the Master and Chief of the young Demons who served him.

The next moment, when the Man in Black shouted, "Ho, ho, young man, what's your hurry? It's time you paid up and I've come to collect what belongs to me," Filippo suddenly realized that everything —in this world or the next—has a price. His soul was the price *he'd* pay for all he received!

Filippo's teeth chattered, his spine tingled and he stood as though rooted to the mosaics under his feet—but not for long. He glanced around wildly and when his eyes fell upon the endless steps to the church, he made a desperate plan. If he could reach the door and slip inside ahead of the Devil, he'd be safe. Once inside the sanctuary, neither Satan nor all the Demons of Hell could touch him!

How Filippo carried out his scheme, he never knew. For no sooner had he started to race up the steps than the Man in Black shrieked at his heels, "I wouldn't try that. No one escapes from the Devil!" He'd almost touched the youth's jacket with a dark bony finger when Filippo slammed the door on the leering face.

"Thank you, dear Lord," gasped Filippo, sinking in a heap on the floor. He tried hard to pray, but discovered to his horror the words jumbled strangely, he couldn't remember what to say. Then, all at once, he remembered he'd not prayed since he'd read his great-uncle's book!

All that day Filippo tried to pray. The hour waxed late. The jewel colors faded from the great rose window, ghostlike shadows filled the long aisles and the candles on the altar sputtered. Beads of sweat stood out on the youth's brow when he cried desperately, "Help me, dear Lord. The Devil waits without to snatch my soul. I have no refuge, no h-hope."

As Filippo's voice trailed off in despair, the Abbot—who was keeping late vigil—heard his cry, went to his side and placed a hand on the shaking shoulder. "With God, there always is hope for the repentant sinner," the old man said kindly.

But after the youth gradually poured out the story of the book, how he'd been practicing sorcery and the Devil had come to collect his soul, in return for benefits he'd received, the Abbot looked grave. Before making a reply, he fingered the gold cross on his breast, sighed deeply and pulled at his beard. "Your sin is grievous, my son," said he at last. "I must take you at once to the Pope. Only he can decide what you must do to save your soul."

But when the Abbot attempted to lead Filippo to the door, the latter drew back. "No, no, Satan is out there," he cried in panic. "I'm safe only here, inside the church."

"You are wrong, my son," said the Abbot and grasped Filippo's hand firmly. "When I hold this holy cross and lead you from this church, you have naught to fear. Then neither Satan nor his cohorts can harm a hair of your head."

At last Filippo consented reluctantly to accompany the Abbot. Even as the good man had said, when he opened the door and led the youth through the streets to the Pope's palace, Satan was powerless. At sight of the cross, he blanched, slunk away shrieking and vanished in a thick cloud of smoke.

When Filippo knelt before the Pope, later, confessed his sins and cried, "Tell me how to save my soul, escape from the Devil and receive forgiveness," the Holy Father was even more grave than the Abbot.

"You have sinned greatly," the Pope said severely. "Only after you do penance, make long pilgrimage and then return for absolution can I do anything for you."

"I'll do anything, go anywhere—if only I can be forgiven," promised Filippo. And then, thinking of the waiting Devil, he blanched. "But—but it's no use," he added disconsolately. "The instant I leave the palace, Satan will s-snatch my soul."

The Pope seemed not to hear. "That path to salvation is rough and the way long," said he. "The only way you can hope to be forgiven is to go to Christendom's two most holy tombs—that of Our Lord, in Jerusalem and Sant-Yago—Saint James the Apostle—at Santiago de Compostela, in Spain. Do penance at each shrine, bring me proof of your pilgrimage—and then we shall speak of absolution."

"But how can I expect to go anywhere—save to Hell?" Filippo wailed, wringing his hands.

"By wearing this reliquary, night and day," said the Pope, rummaging in the folds of his robe. He drew out a small silver box on a silver chain and hung it around Filippo's neck. "It holds a hair from the head of the blessed Jude—the Saint to whom rascals pray for the Impossible," the Pope said. "The relic will protect you from Satan—until you return from your pilgrimage," he added and dismissed the youth with a wave of the hand.

Back at his lodgings, Filippo took books from the shelf and traced his journey on a parchment map. But when he found Jerusalem was fifteen hundred miles southeast of Rome, and Santiago de Compostela, a thousand northwest, he despaired of ever reaching either shrine. "Hem—three thousand miles there and back to one tomb, two thousand to the other—five thousand miles in all. At that rate, I'd be tottering and bent before my penance was done, the Pope dead and I unshriven."

The prospect was so bleak Filippo slumped to a chair, clasped hands behind head and tried to think what to do. Even with a fleet horse to carry him over land, a fast ship at sea and a gale behind, the pilgrimage would take years and years and, most likely, "I'd never return—and yet I must make it," he argued gloomily.

It was not yet quite dawn when Filippo had his splendid idea —the idea that would solve everything. The thought came to him when his eyes fell upon his great-uncle's sheepskin-bound book, lying right there on the table before him. "That's it!" he shouted in excitement and leaped to his feet. "I'll summon a young Devil—this one last time. With his aid—and Saint Jude's—I could make the entire journey, there and back, in a night, the Pope would forgive me tomorrow and—and I'll have the rest of my life to make amends for my crime." But the youth finished uncertainly, for his conscience pricked him. His purpose was pure. Surely the end justified the means, he told himself uneasily.

But despite his uneasiness, Filippo clapped his hands, back to back. The next instant, there stood three young grinning Devils, with horns on their heads, wings on their shoulders and long jaunty tails. "What does the Master desire?" they asked mockingly, bowing from their slim waists.

"To go to Jerusalem, in the Holy Land—then on to Santiago de Compostela, in Spain—and be back in Rome by this time tomorrow," Filippo said and asked which Devil could fly fastest.

"Ho, ho, need you ask?" snorted the Shortest Devil, elbowing the others out of the way. "*I* fly fast as the wind."

"Which isn't fast enough," Filippo said. "Even the fastest wind can't blow a ship through the Mediterranean in a night."

"Then try *me!*" shrilled the Middle-Sized Devil. "I'm faster than sound."

"That's not fast enough, either," Filippo objected. "Before the sound of my voice can echo in a cave, I have a thousand thoughts."

"Thoughts, eh? Then I'm your fellow!" roared the Tallest Devil gleefully, kicking his companions aside. "*I* fly fast as thought."

"Then come here," Filippo ordered. "Take me with all speed to the Church of the Holy Sepulcher, in Jerusalem."

Without further ado, Filippo climbed to the Tallest Devil's shoulders, prodded his ribs sharply and shouted, "Off with you, then—and mind you don't dawdle."

The Tallest Devil *didn't* dawdle. For good as his word, he skimmed, quicker than thought, high over the blue Mediterranean, the ruined temples of Greece and the jewel isles of the Aegean. Then above the rolling hills of Palestine he soared, circled the sky over the Holy Sepulcher Church and swiftly descended, within the Holy City's lofty walls. "Well done," gasped Filippo. Then he slid from the Devil's back and ordered him to await his return.

Filippo entered the church immediately, knelt long at the sacred tomb and prayed earnestly, "Forgive my sins, dear Lord, save my soul from Satan's clutches and teach me to live in repentance and peace."

When Filippo rose, he felt strangely comforted. And, as he left the church, his heart was lighter than when he entered. But his penance wasn't done—not until he'd followed the winding street—the Via Dolorosa—people say Our Lord trod on His way to Calvary. Along the via, the youth stopped at each Station of the Cross, lighted a taper and prayed for the souls of the dead.

Next, Filippo set about seeking a memento of his pilgrimage, "To prove to the Pope I've made it," he said, and visited the city's dusty shops and crowded marts. When he found a small olive wood cross— "fashioned of the tree where Christ knelt, in Gethsemane," he was told —he bought it at great price.

What the merchant *didn't* say was that the relic, though made of Gethsemane wood, was unblessed. Otherwise, the waiting Devil would have vanished when Filippo returned! But as it was, the youth smiled happily, wrapped the cross in a kerchief and slipped it inside his shirtfront. And when he climbed to the Demon's back and directed, "Take me to Santiago de Compostela, in the northwest tip of Spain," he obeyed instantly.

And now, though the distance was greater, the Devil flew faster and arrived sooner at his destination than before. He'd barely flapped his dark leathery wings, mounted the sky and faced the northwest than he was above the Mediterranean, then Sardinia and finally the desolate barren plateau of Spain.

When at last the Devil zoomed to the square before the cathedral, Filippo, too breathless to speak, slipped to his feet. Then he hurried forward to join a group of pilgrims who, with lighted tapers, formed in procession and pressed toward the church.

Inch by inch, the procession advanced until it reached the tomb in the crypt—the tomb that a miraculous star reputedly revealed as holy Sant-Yago's last resting place.

At the tomb, as before, Filippo clasped his hands, bowed his head and prayed. "Dear Sant-Yago, save me from Satan and deliver my soul from sin," he petitioned. When he rose, he gave lavishly to the church, the poor and lighted three-times-twenty candles for the souls of the dead. "Give them peace, dear Lord," he prayed.

And then, as before, Filippo sought for a memento to take back to the Pope. When the youth found an old wrinkled woman at a stall, selling cockleshells—the badge of pilgrims to Santiago de Compostela—his eyes shone. "Take this, kind Grandmother," he said, pressing a piece of gold in the crone's hand. "May it bless you as your shell will bless me," he said, thinking of the Holy Father's forgiveness.

Filippo wrapped the shell in the kerchief, along with the cross, stuffed the treasures inside his shirt and returned to the Devil.

But early next day, at the palace, Filippo was doomed to bitter disappointment. For when he knelt before the Pope, laid the objects on his palm and said, "Here is proof of my pilgrimage to the holy tombs," the old man stared coldly. And when the youth, unaware of his displeasure, rushed on confidently, "I have fulfilled your requirements, Holy Father, done penance at the shrines of Our Saviour and the blessed Sant-Yago, and now return once more to ask forgiveness," the Pope drew back in horror.

"How dare you—" the Pope thundered, shaking with rage. "How dare you ask forgiveness? Only one in league with Satan could make a pilgrimage of five thousand miles in a single night! Yet you bring these relics, ask absolution and say you repent!"

"But I *do!*" cried Filippo, his face falling and his head spinning. "Besides, I meant no harm. When I saw how far I'd have to travel, how many years it would take and how old I'd be when I finished my pilgrimage—if I did—I decided to call on a Devil to help me, for the last time," he stumbled on desperately. "Otherwise, I'd have no time left to show my repentance was real. But now," he ended dejectedly, "now S-Satan—"

"Will take your soul," finished the Pope with a harsh laugh. "You can't expect forgiveness when you make a pilgrimage that costs neither hardship nor effort, and but a single night in time! Don't expect forgiveness from me—or anyone on earth—for sins such as yours."

So saying, the Holy Father averted his face, gathered his white robe about him and swept from the room. Even after his footsteps died in the corridor, the dreadful words echoed in Filippo's mind. Sobbing and crushed, he knelt before the empty chair and clutched at the relic around his neck. "Even you, Saint Jude, can't help me now," he moaned dully.

It was late, when Filippo finally lifted his head and saw the crucifix on the wall. The palace was silent, the audience chamber dark and a moonbeam from the window bathed the gentle face on the cross in soft radiant light. All at once, the young man stretched his arms and cried in anguish, "Please, dear Lord in Heaven, help me. What with no forgiveness on earth, where can I, a sinner, turn save to You?"

When the One on the Cross stirred, the lips moved and He uttered the words, "My son, *I* forgive you," great peace filled Filippo's soul.

"Thus, at last, Filippo Pipetta found grace," the old legend tells us. "From the moment he received forgiveness, he was a changed man."

The first thing he did was return to his lodgings, burn his great-uncle's book on witchcraft and resume his study of the stars. In time, Filippo became one of the great astronomers of his day, married a beautiful girl and was honored and loved. "Thanks to Saint Jude, who grants the Impossible," Filippo told his wife.

And as for the Pope—who couldn't see the sinner's heart beyond his sin—*he*, also, changed. For when he learned Our Lord had forgiven the man to whom he, the Holy Father, denied absolution, he hung his head in shame. Through penitence and prayer he humbled his spirit, until at last, he became a kind and just man.

11   THE REPENTANT FOX
(Ireland)

For hundreds of years, in hundreds of ways, early Gaelic monks recorded the tender tale of Saint Kiaran and his Beasts on flyleaves and margins of their holy books. Later, when more learned scribes wrote *their* accounts of the Saints—in Latin on huge parchment tomes—they embellished on these simple heart-warming tales. That's why—what with time and well-meaning monks writing many times of the same event—facts were often scrambled. Some scribes even claimed that Saint Kiaran lived a hundred years *after* the great Saint Patrick.

Of course, this is not so at all. *Both* Saints lived in the fifth century. One was old, the other young. They were friends and met on the road outside Rome, the very day this story began.

That was the proudest day in Saint Kiaran's life. After studying the Scriptures twenty years in Rome, the Pope had made him Bishop and commanded him to return to his native Erin. "Preach there to the pagan chieftains, convert them and baptize their people in the name of Christ," the Holy Father charged.

Saint Kiaran lost no time in carrying out his orders. He set forth at once on his long journey, taking naught save a begging bowl and staff, the robe on his back and the sandals on his feet. He'd gone barely seven miles from Rome when he met his friend, the young monk, Patrick, striding toward the Eternal City.

"We meet by God's holy plan," Saint Patrick exclaimed, after the monks had blessed each other, embraced and kissed as Brothers in Christ. "Last night in a dream, He sent His Angel to command me to go to Rome to study for the priesthood, give you a message and this bell."

Thereupon, the young monk rummaged in the folds of his robe, drew forth a bell, strangely wrought with birds and beasts, and placed it on Saint Kiaran's palm. "It shall be your guide and fellow traveler on your journey," said Saint Patrick, smiling at the astonishment on his companion's face. "The bell has wondrous powers."

"But—" Saint Kiaran stammered, staring at the rich gleaming bell. " 'Tis more a fitting companion to an Emperor in ermine than a poor wayfaring priest like me."

"God thinks otherwise!" Saint Patrick said and went on to explain that his teacher, Bishop Germanus, had given him the bell when he completed his studies. " 'Cherish it,' the old man charged. ' 'Tis not like other bells. One day its voice shall lead a holy man to the small cold spring, called Fuaran, deep in the forest, in the heart of Erin.' When I pressed him to learn more, the Bishop shook his head. 'God shall reveal all—in time,' he said. And last night He did," Patrick concluded.

"But what has the bell to do with me?" asked Saint Kiaran, more puzzled than ever.

"*You* are the holy man!" Saint Patrick replied, his arm about his friend's shoulders.

"But Fuaran—in the forest—at Erin's heart," mused Saint Kiaran, pulling at his beard. "I know my country as well as the wrinkles on my face—yet I've not heard of the place of the spring. Where is it, and how can I find it?" he asked.

"The place you seek lies on the border 'twixt the Men of the North and the Men of the South, the Angel told me." Saint Patrick said. "The bell shall lead you thither. It shall be voiceless until you approach Fuaran. Then it shall ring loud and clear. There God wills you to build a cell, gather Disciples and found a Holy House. And there, dear Brother," he concluded, smiling, "I shall join you—thirty years hence."

"And I, with God's grace, your prayers and this holy bell, shall find the place," Saint Kiaran said resolutely and fastened the bell to the cord at his waist.

Thus, after once more blessing each other, the holy men parted, Saint Kiaran going to the north and Saint Patrick to the south.

How many months, or even years, it took to make the perilous journey over the high Alps, through forests and across valleys, Saint Kiaran didn't know. But make the journey he did. And when he'd crossed the sea and reached his native land, he met with hardship, hunger and hostile pagan tribesmen. Yet—despite ebbing strength and many disappointments—his courage never flagged. "In God's good time, the bell will speak," he told himself.

Yet, as the days passed, it did not speak. No matter how many times the Saint crisscrossed the countryside he knew so well, he couldn't find the boundary between the Men of the North and the Men of the South. The bell held its tongue. Then one day, when he was so spent he thought he could go no farther, the miracle happened.

When Saint Kiaran lifted his eyes and gazed about—lo!—there was a forest he'd not seen before. Leaning heavily on his staff, he stumbled forward. He'd barely taken one, then two, and finally, three steps, when he felt a quivering at his side. Glancing down, he saw the bell move. Then it swung violently and finally it rang. So sweet and clear was its voice that the holy man—dazed as he was with weariness—thought at first, he was dead, in Heaven and listening to the Angels, ringing the bells of Paradise.

At each advancing step the bell rang more clearly. But at last, when it stopped suddenly as it started, the Saint knew he was alive, had reached the heart of Erin and the bell had brought him to the spring. "Thank you, thank you, dear Lord," he cried, dropping to his knees. It was then he heard the soft burblings 'neath the long grasses at his side.

"That's how Saint Kiaran found Fuaran," wrote the early monks in their huge parchment tomes. "And when he'd praised God, blessed the bell and drunk deeply of the holy spring, he waxed strong again."

As the Saint rested beside the spring, he planned happily. "Here I'll build a cell, as the Angel directed, and a shrine to the bell. But as for gathering Disciples in this wilderness—only you, dear Lord, can guide me in that."

And this the dear Lord did. For barely had the Saint spoken when he heard fearsome snortings, snufflings and grunts. He saw, peering at him through the underbrush, a beast's small frightened eyes, and the next instant, a wild boar, with long snout and sharp tusks, rushed past to a clump of oaks nearby.

"Come back, little one," murmured the Saint. "I'll not harm you—though I daresay your first glimpse of a two-legged Beast is terrifying."

Thereupon, Saint Kiaran, who knew that Beasts, like men, are inquisitive, waited patiently. Before long the Boar conquered his fear, crept back, snout to ground, and sniffed noisily at the motionless creature. When the holy man slowly reached a hand toward the rough head, rubbed the ears gently and said, "Fear not, little one, we are friends," the animal edged closer, with a pleased grunt.

And friends they were from that moment—the Saint and the wild Boar. Love sprang up between them. And when the Beast saw the kindness in the old man's face, felt the warmth of his hand and the power of his presence, his heart filled with strange longing. "Let me live with you, serve you and learn your ways," he cried, lifting his fierce-looking head and gazing into the eyes of his new friend.

"So you shall, Brother Boar," replied the Saint joyfully, for all at once the meaning of the Angel's command was clear. "You shall be my first Disciple. We shall labor together, share all things and I shall teach you."

That was the beginning of the hermitage in the forest. For Brother Boar served the holy man as monk serves abbot, obeyed him and struggled against his savage ways.

The first thing Brother Boar did, was help build the cell beside the spring. With his sharp tusks, he uprooted hassocks of grass and dug stones from the riverbed. With his strong teeth he tore branches from trees and ripped away bark. Then, his materials gathered, he fetched them to the Saint. He in turn, built a snug cell, with wattle-and-mud walls, a well-sodded roof—and even a hearth and stone floor.

Last of all, Saint Kiaran fashioned a ledge for the bell and placed spring flowers—wood violets and anemones—beside it. Then he knelt, gave thanks once more, for the miracle that led him to the well, and brought him his first Disciple.

Word of how a wild boar had gone to live with the holy man spread through the forest from Beast to Beast. Now others besought him to let them dwell with him. "Pray let me serve you, holy Saint," entreated a Stag, who knocked one day at his door. "I hear you teach a gentler law than that of the forest."

"You are right, my friend," replied the Saint. "The law of Christ forbids killing our brothers, commands us to live together in peace and grow in grace."

"Teach me, good Saint. Let me serve you," the Stag begged, kneeling before the holy man.

After the Stag, other Beasts of the wild implored Saint Kiaran to admit them to his brotherhood. The lean gray Wolf, the clever Badger—and even the red Fox with handsome brush and cunning eyes —scratched at the door of the cell. He received them joyfully. "You shall be my Disciples; we shall share everything and abstain from flesh."

As time passed, the little band was happy. Thanks to the Saint's wisdom, the wild Beasts grew tame. They loved their Abbot, strove to obey him, and each had his duties. Some fetched wood; others gathered food—berries, nuts and tender roots—for their common table. All drank the refreshing waters of the spring. And all, in turn, guarded the hermitage, when their Abbot was absent in the forest.

Yet Beasts, like men, alas, can fall from grace. Such was the case with poor Brother Fox. In the forest, he'd lived by cunning and theft. At the hermitage, he found it hard to change his ways. Some Brothers eyed him with suspicion—though the Saint always understood.

Once, a fellow monk caught the Fox licking a sheepskin-bound prayer book, dragged him to the Saint and accused him of meaning to chew it. "And who are you to impute evil motives to Brother Fox?" asked the old man sternly and dismissed the culprit with an encouraging smile.

After that, Brother Fox tried harder and did better—till the day he found and ate the honeycomb Brother Boar planned for supper. When the Boar saw the Fox's sticky whiskers, he grunted, "Once a thief, always a thief!" and turned his broad back.

Guilt rested heavily on Brother Fox. At last, he went to the Saint, knelt before him and confessed everything. "I've s-sinned again," he ended.

"We all do, Brother Fox," said the holy man, his eyes twinkling. "Now get up, you wretch," he added severely. "And mind you don't steal your Brothers' supper again."

And Brother Fox didn't. Indeed, he was such a changed Beast that, one proud day, Saint Kiaran said, "It's your turn to guard the hermitage, while we go to the forest."

"Have no fear, dear Master," cried the Fox joyfully. "I'll look well to everything." And no sooner had the Saint, followed by the Boar, the Stag, the Wolf, and the Badger, disappeared among the trees than Brother Fox set to work to prove himself.

He swept the cell floor, dusted the bench with a swipe of his tail and placed buttercups and daisies on the ledge before the bell. Then he fetched fresh boughs of fir for the Saint's couch.

It was only when Brother Fox paused, wondering what to do next, that he caught the scent of untanned leather that made his nose itch. Then he saw the Saint's sandals in the corner.

"No, no, I'll not touch them," Brother Fox told himself in alarm. "They've been there all the while. I was too busy to notice," he added and shut his eyes tightly. But with his eyes closed, the scent of hide only plagued his nose more. The harder he tried not to think about the leather, the greater was his desire to gnaw it.

When his mouth drooled and his whiskers twitched, he knew it was no use. With a despairing growl, Brother Fox snatched up the sandals, bolted from the door and loped toward his old den in the wild.

When the Saint returned with his Disciples, sometime later, glanced about quickly and found both the Fox—and the sandals—gone, his heart was heavy. "Why should Brother Fox do this evil thing?" he asked sadly.

"Because he's never changed, that's why," grunted Brother Boar meanly, thinking of the honeycomb. "In the old days, Brother Fox took what he chose and fared better than most of us."

"We all have our faults, Brother Boar," the Saint retorted so sharply the Beast hung his head in shame. *His* fault was gluttony! Yet how often, when they'd had his favorite nuts for supper, had the kind Abbot pushed over his share, saying that such foods were too rich for an old man!

But now the Stag was speaking. "The smell of the leather reminded Brother Fox of the meat he used to eat," he comforted. "A sudden impulse overcame him."

"It's hard to change old ways for new," said Brother Wolf, with so much feeling the others stared.

"But it's not as if Brother Fox didn't *try*." The Saint sighed. "He'll return soon, bring back the sandals and make amends," he added with more confidence than he felt.

But the monks shook their heads. Brother Boar was first to speak, and this time, there was concern in his voice. "One of us should go after him," he said. "I'd go, but am no match for him when he's roused."

"I'd not even know where to look for his den," said Brother Stag. "In the forest I always avoided him."

"And well you did," the Wolf rumbled. "Before Brother Fox was a Christian monk, he was ferocious and—"

"Please, dear Saint, let me go," interrupted the Badger, speaking for the first time. "I know where to find Brother Fox, what to say when I do and how to bring him back to repentance—with your sandals, too, I daresay."

The Saint pulled at his beard, stared thoughtfully at the badger's long curved claws and replied reluctantly, "Very well, dear Brother, you may go and our prayers will go with you. But take care. You are small, the Fox short-tempered, so I've heard—and who knows what might happen? But mind this," the holy man added sternly. "You're not to use those needle-sharp claws."

The Badger laughed softly before replying, "I'll not need to. Brother Fox already knows how sharp they are! That's why he'll listen when I speak. And have no fear, dear Saint," he ended. "I can take care of myself. I know the ways of the forest at night and where to find our brother's lair."

The moon hung in the sky like a silver ball, when Brother Badger took his leave, trundled into the forest on his short legs and sniffed his way toward the river. There he crossed the flat bridge of stones, turned up a slope and clambered cautiously toward a rocky ledge. By peering down, he could see the dark yawning mouth of the den.

The beast cocked his short ears, listened intently and, when he heard sounds of something being dragged over rough stones, grinned shrewdly. Then, "*Hem!*" Brother Badger cleared his throat mightily, and listened again. But when no sound issued from the den—only a stillness thicker than a thundercloud—the Beast bellowed, "Ho, Brother Fox, can you hear me?" so loudly the rocks echoed. "The Saint has sent me to fetch you home—along with his sandals—if you haven't devoured them already."

When a low angry growl was the Badger's only answer, he threatened, "If you don't come out with the sandals at once, things will go hard with you. I'll—"

"You'll *what?*" rasped the Fox, his voice muffled. For even as the Beast spoke, he'd torn a bit off one sandal toe and was trying to chew the hide. But the leather was old and hard, and so dry it nearly choked him. "I'll bring out the sandals when I c-choose. I only meant to *borrow* them a-anyway," he finished with a desperate gulp.

"Liar and thief! Borrow them, eh? A likely tale! You'll bring them *now*—if you're wise," roared the Badger so fiercely the Fox blanched. "If you don't, I'll come in for them myself. And then, my friend, I'll crop your ears, scratch out your whiskers and as for that brush, ha—when I'm finished with *that*, it will look like a rat's tail!"

By now the Badger was shaking with laughter, but Brother Fox didn't know it. *He* was alarmed. Mustering what dignity he could, he replied in a tone of injured innocence, "Very well, Brother Badger, have it your way. Since you're making an uproar over a pair of old sandals, I may as well return them now as later."

"*Better*," thundered the Badger, "if you know what's good for you."

Thereupon Brother Fox grabbed the sandals in his teeth—making sure the chewed toe didn't show—ambled into the moonlight and snarled sullenly. "Well, here I am—and so are the sandals. And since you're in such a hurry, we'd best start at once. Some clumsy beasts need a long time to get anywhere," he added meanly, staring at the Badger's short stubby legs.

"And some need a long time to ponder their ingratitude," retorted the Badger. "You'd best follow me, Brother Fox—tail between legs and head bowed in shame—and think well what you'll say to the dear Saint. After he taught you, gave you a home and shared all he had, he couldn't trust you a few hours to guard his possessions! For shame!"

Brother Fox didn't reply at once to the harsh words. When he did, he moaned, "I—I love the dear Saint more than the others. I've fallen from grace more times, he's understood how hard I tried and forgiven me more often—but n-now—" his voice trailed off wretchedly.

"Now he'll forgive you again," said the Badger gently. And when he turned in the moonlight and added, "We'll all forgive you, dear Brother," the sharp face was kind.

And this all the Brothers did. For back at the hermitage, when the erring Fox laid the sandals at his Master's feet, confirmed the tale of how the smell of untanned leather had tempted him and asked forgiveness, the Saint understood. And so did the monks—even Brother Boar.

"I'm done with stealing," the Fox contritely promised. "I'll do penance, I'll not eat—not so much as to snap a fly—till you give permission. And as for your sandals," he added anxiously, "I only gnawed the tip of one toe. I don't think I harmed them—much."

A smile quirked at the corners of the Saint's lips. "I'm sure you didn't, dear Brother Fox," said he, rubbing the repentant creature's pointed ears. "Return the sandals to the corner and ask Our dear Lord to forgive you. I have already."

The repentant Fox started his fast, next day. He refused food until the Abbot bade him eat, prayed for grace—and received it—and in time became a model monk. Indeed, in time he grew into such an honest and reliable Beast, his fellow Disciples declared, "You can always depend on Brother Fox."

The old tale goes on to say that after those first happy years with his Beast Disciples, wise men from many lands knocked at the door of the hermitage in the forest. "Teach us, Holy Saint," they entreated. "Let us live with you, sit at your feet and learn to be Christian monks."

To this Saint Kiaran gave happy consent. "The words of the Angel are fulfilled," he told his Disciples. And such was the case, for thus the great monastery of olden times, Saigir, had its beginning. For many years the Holy House flourished—though now, alas, after fifteen centuries, only its memory remains.

After thirty years Saint Patrick, true to his promise, joined his friend, the Abbot of Saigir, at Fuaran, the small cold spring in the forest. Together they labored, preached the Word and baptized Erin's chieftains and heathen tribes. And years later, after the great Kiaran died, men proclaimed Bishop Patrick the Patron Saint of the land.

And as for the holy bell—the folk of the countryside regarded that with reverence. "Its voice is the Voice of God," they said. For long years they carried the precious thing on procession, when the chieftains took oath, the poor wanted alms or the monastery tithes. Far and wide, the people called the bell "Kiaran's *bardan*."

No one knows now, after so many years, where the bardan is. To this day, the old folk cross themselves at its mention. " 'Tis somewhere at the green heart of Erin," they explain. Then they go on to speak of the Beasts—the Wolf and the Boar, the Stag and the Badger—and the repentant Fox.

"Of all his monks, Saint Kiaran loved them most," say the Old Ones. "Even when Saigir was powerful, rich and men from many parts went there, he kept his dear Beasts with him. Till they died of old age he cherished them, had them at his side and taught them in ways of Christian brotherhood."

12   THE CLOAK OF
SAINT BEATUS
(Switzerland)

Legend tells us that the Apostle to Switzerland, holy Saint Beatus, arrived one day on the east shore of Thunersee—the Lake of Thun—and preached the Word to the heathen tribes roundabout.

Who the Saint was or whence he came, no one seems to know, now that nine hundred years have passed. Some say he crossed the Irish Sea, the high Alps and finally arrived at Thunersee by miraculous means. Others pooh at the idea. "He lived no farther away than the timber-built village of Lungern," they say, pointing to the northeast.

A few dare insist there were *two* Saints named Beatus. Time—which has a way of tricking the memory—has confused one with the other, they claim. And *they* say the Great Apostle had naught to do with the Saint of our story!

We know this is nonsense. Only the muddle-headed could confuse our Saint with another. But all that matters is that Saint Beatus did arrive at Thunersee—without worldly possessions save for his tall staff and old worn cloak. He found a grotto high in the rocks, and lived there, many years, as a hermit. His heart burned with such missionary zeal that, despite hunger, hardship and hostile tribesmen, he won countless souls to Christ. When his fellow worker, Saint Justus, joined him, later, he already had many friends. So we might say, there *were* two Saints, but one came after the other.

111

Indeed, to know Saint Beatus, was to love him, we're told. To hear his gay laughter quickened hope in the heart, and when he preached, everyone—from the greatest to the least—hoarded each golden word, as a miser hoards treasure.

When the Saint spoke of the Loving One who demands the heart, rather than human sacrifice, the people forsook their cruel gods of stone and wood. As the years came and went, they destroyed their bloodstained altars, built churches and adorned them with care. Within there were rich carvings. They crowned the slender steeples with Christian crosses.

God prospered the labors of the two missionaries. In time, the crosses marked both shores of the Lake of Thun. And now, what with visiting the old, encouraging the young and watching over the new parishes—especially Aeschi, on the far side of the lake—the two Saints, Beatus and Justus, had more work to do than hours in the day to do it. Had it not been for the help of a faithful convert, the old Chieftain Ners, they would have done less.

One night, at supper, Saint Beatus rolled his eyes in mock despair. "If only Our Lord had made me twins," he groaned, "I'd do twice the work, reach Aeschi in half the time and double our lambs in the fold. It takes so long to get anywhere in our little boat."

Saint Justus, who was solemn as his companion gay, didn't approve of such levity. He averted his face, coughed and said stiffly, "When Our Lord wishes you to get there faster, I'm sure He will show the way."

Saint Beatus' eyes twinkled. "I'm sure He will," he said. "But remember, meanwhile, dear Brother, the Lord loves a cheerful heart," and he bade Justus good night.

Next day, Beatus had barely finished prayers, when a messenger from Aeschi, across the lake, brought word that the ailing Ners had worsened, was calling his name and begging his presence.

Without losing a minute, the Saint wrapped himself in his cloak, snatched up his staff and hurried down the steep slope. "Don't let me fail him, dear Lord," he prayed as he leaped from rock to rock. "Let me reach him in time to give absolution." To cross the two-mile-wide lake in a frail boat took time.

Just as Beatus reached the bank and stooped to untie the skiff, a freakish wind ripped off his cloak. When he turned to grab it, it flapped out of reach, landed on the blue water and then spread out in an extraordinary manner. Instead of bunching, sinking or lying in a sodden mass, it lay flat—flat as sunbaked earth. *"Mmm—mm,"* mused the hermit, pulling at his beard. The longer he stared at the cloak, the odder it seemed that it should lie there spread out, for no special reason.

All at once Saint Beatus threw back his head and laughed till his mirth echoed like music across the wide lake, swept through the trees on the shore and floated above the pasturelands. "Thank you, thank you, dear Lord," he cried, when able to speak. "Saint Justus was right. You *have* shown me a way to cross more quickly."

Thereupon, without hesitation, Saint Beatus leaped to the middle of his cloak, seated himself and pushed off with his tall staff. Then the miracle happened! The garment glided off swiftly—more swiftly than an eagle, more nimbly than a hind pursued by huntsmen and quicker than thought. When the cloak arrived at the bank opposite, the Saint jumped ashore, climbed up the ridge and entered the Chieftain's hut.

Gazing down at the wan wasted face, the Saint feared, at first, he had arrived too late. But when the old man stirred feebly, groped for his hand and then tried to speak his name, Beatus knew all was well. "Thank you, dear Lord, for bringing me in time," he whispered, as the Chieftain drifted into sleep, a smile on his lips.

From that day, old Ners rallied. As strength returned to his body, so did a burning zest to finish the church he'd helped his people begin. It would be the most beautiful and complete sanctuary for miles about, he confided to the missionaries, who doubled their efforts to help the struggling parish.

And now that Beatus, thanks to the miracle, could sit on his cloak, paddle with his staff and reach the far side of the lake whenever there was a need, he made the trip often. Soon he was doing the work of ten. But all the while, he said nothing of his adventure to his solemn fellow hermit. Rubbing his hands gleefully, the Saint said, "Justus might think my mode of travel unbecoming to a missionary!" and kept his own counsel.

That's why the two holy men, both laboring at Aeschi, came and went at separate times, each in his own way. God blessed their labors and the small timber church high on the ridge—with the Kandor Valley on one side, Thunersee on the other—was indeed the most beautiful house of worship for miles around. With loving care the folk of Aeschi carved the high pulpit with fruits and flowers of the region. They chipped a font from Alpine granite. "Our church shall be a shining beacon," old Ners gloated, as the edifice neared completion.

At last, the church at Aeschi was finished. It was mid-August, the weather uncommonly hot and the time of dedication at hand. "Come Sunday, you shall preach our first sermon," the Chieftain told Saint Beatus proudly. "We'll have more worshipers than ever you've preached to before, more candles on the altar and garlands of flowers."

Saint Beatus listened uneasily to the old man's boasts. "Take care, dear friend," the hermit said. "Once pride enters through the church door, the Evil One creeps in unseen."

Dedication Sunday dawned hot. Bees buzzed above the clover patches, birds drowsed in the trees and Saint Beatus—who'd spent the night on his knees—must have been wool-gathering. He left the grotto, hurried down the steep rocky path and got as far as Rudi's pasture without missing his staff.

The Saint probably wouldn't have thought of it then, if his gaze hadn't fallen on the cowherd's new fence. It was when pausing to admire the long slender rails—and the skill with which he had woven them together—that Beatus remembered his staff. "How stupid can a body be?" he cried, clapping hand to brow. "Without it, I can't steer my course. If I go back to fetch it now, I'll be late!"

Fortunately, Justus had gone on ahead, to see all was in readiness. But for Beatus to be late for saying Holy Mass was unthinkable!

It was while pondering what to do that he glanced at the fence a second time. One of those long smooth stakes might serve almost as well as his staff, he decided, not thinking of the miraculous power with which God had endowed it. Besides, the hermit reasoned, if he pulled out a rail carefully, no one—even Rudi—would be the wiser and he'd return it on the way home.

But God was the wiser, and no stick could be the same as one He blessed—as Saint Beatus should have known. Moments later, he'd spread out the cloak, sat down, as usual, and tried to push off with the borrowed stake. Then everything happened at once.

The cloak tipped first this side, then that, and when Saint Beatus tried cautiously to steer, the edges puffed up. When they'd risen so high he couldn't see where he was, he tried poking with the stake. It was then the garment flapped in anger, flounced toward the middle of Thunersee and spun around and around like a Dervish. Next, as though bewitched, the cloak tried to drown the terrified Saint.

There's no telling what might have happened, if Saint Beatus hadn't realized, all at once, what he'd done. When the cloak gave such a dizzy dip he thought his last hour had come, he cried humbly, "Dear Lord, forgive me. I was presumptuous. I thought any stick would do as well as the one You chose for a miracle. Moreover, this stake I hold belongs to another. I had no right to take it—and now it's too l-late to—"

But nothing, with God, is too late. No sooner were the words spoken than the garment righted itself. It sped swiftly to shore. And when Saint Beatus had replaced the rail in Rudi's fence, returned to the grotto and fetched his own staff, his cloak carried him safely across the two-mile-wide lake.

But now it was late. By the time Saint Beatus had trudged up the ridge and reached the church it was so late that Saint Justus, thinking he'd met with mishap, had already said the Mass, chanted the responses and begun the sermon.

But the good man, alas, pious and beloved though he was, was no preacher. As his words, leaden and heavy as Saint Beatus' were golden, poured forth in a dull stream, his listeners, one by one, were overcome with a longing to sleep. And what with the church so crowded, the day hot—and the monotonous buzz of a fly—every man, woman and child nodded or twitched. Old Ners slept soundly.

When Saint Beatus opened the door, stepped within and saw the bobbing heads, he flushed with anger. *Slothful little ones,* he thought. *Have I labored among you so long to see such shamelessness?*

As Saint Beatus tiptoed down the aisle toward the empty seat near the font, the members of the congregation were too drowsy to see him. And Saint Justus, too engrossed in his words to be aware of aught else, droned on.

On reaching his place, Saint Beatus bowed his head in despair. If he interrupted the Holy Service and roused the people, he'd be irreverent. But to let them sleep imperiled their souls.

At length the Saint lifted his head and glanced around anxiously. Now at least a dozen more heads bobbed. At least a dozen more worshipers slept. Just as he was wondering what he'd best do, Beatus caught sight of the swarthy Devil with bright bulgy eyes, who lolled at ease on the floor—between the pulpit and the font.

The blood froze in Saint Beatus' veins and his ruddy face blanched whiter than the Matterhorn's snows, when he saw what Satan was doing. With a frowsy black crow-feather quill, he was scratching names on a goat-hide parchment—the names of the worshipers, one by one, who succumbed to sleep. The horns on the ugly fellow's head quivered with excitement, the leer on his lips deepened and his tail twitched gleefully as the list lengthened and the space on the hide lessened.

The Saint watched with horror as the quill in the dreadful claw hand scratched on and on. As he well knew unless he acted quickly, the Devil would claim the souls of the unwary ones, drag them off and burn them like chaff in the fires of Hell. Yet how to thwart the awful plan, drive the Fiend from the church and save the folk of Aeschi, Saint Beatus didn't know—not, at least, until events took the odd twist that changed everything.

When the Devil's list was so long there wasn't room on the hide for even a comma, his greedy eyes roved over the church like search-lights. And when they picked out still more sleepers, he decided to

stretch out the parchment. That was when Satan stuck the quill behind his ear. And then, holding one end of the hide in his teeth and the other in his claw hands, he pulled.

The Devil pulled the hide longer and longer, and the longer he pulled it, the thinner it grew. But that, in his frenzy to get more room, he didn't notice. Saint Beatus edged forward on his seat, when Satan finally braced his back next the pulpit, his cloven feet next to the font, and stretched the parchment with all the power of his long skinny arms.

Then *Ziss—SSS—TTT*! Like thin shattering ice, the taut goat-skin split. The Devil, his balance lost, lurched forward so suddenly, the crow feather sailed from his ear and he banged his head on the font as hard as a blacksmith bangs hammer on nail. A lump the size of a goose egg quickly rose 'twixt his two trembling horns.

Now the cocky Devil's plight was so silly that Saint Beatus—be it said to his shame—couldn't help laughing. "Ho, ho, ho—oho—ha, ha." He laughed so heartily that the sleepers, from the oldest to the young-est, woke with a start. Saint Justus stopped his sermon in the middle of a word and blinked down solemnly at what he saw.

For now the Saint leaped from his seat, brandished his staff and thrashed the Devil within an inch of his life. "Take this—and *this*—and THIS," bellowed Beatus, laying on blows thick and fast. "Get back to Hell and never return—unless you want worse," he added.

The people gaped when, moments later, they saw the Devil stagger to his feet and limp down the aisle. But when at last, Saint Beatus booted out Satan and slammed the door on his dragging tail, they crowded around their beloved priest. Some kissed his hand, others the hem of his robe. Still others reached to touch him.

"Your laughter woke us. It saved us from the Devil's power," the people chanted in gratitude, after Saint Beatus chided them for their sloth, told them how Satan had crept among them as they slept and written their names on his goat hide. "Forgive us. We have sinned," they cried and sank to their knees.

"And forgive me," said Saint Justus humbly. "I have sinned

more than they. I made them sleep. I was too engrossed in my own words to see the Evil One enter our midst."

"We have all sinned—I most of all," Saint Beatus confessed, an arm about Justus' shoulders. "For interrupting your sermon to drive out the Devil, God may forgive me. But to laugh at another's misfortune—even the Devil's—was cruel and unkind. For that sin, I shall do penance," he concluded and hung his head in shame.

Now even as Saint Beatus was talking to his people, legend says that Satan—screaming with pain and smarting with rage at the bagful of souls he'd lost—stumbled down the ridge to the shore of the Lake of Thun. "There angry waves reached to meet him, licked at his cloven feet and pulled him down, down, into the black whirling waters," the folk of Aeschi declare, adding, "For—lo!—these nine hundred years, Satan has not returned. It must be, he remembers the beating our Great Apostle gave him!"

And speaking of the Apostle, when you ask what befell him, after the day he laughed at the Devil's misfortune, the people of Aeschi smile tenderly. "Our Saint Beatus lived and labored in these parts many years thereafter. But for being unkind, God rebuked him. From that day, He took the miraculous power from his cloak and his staff. Whenever the Saint wanted to make the trip from one side of the lake to the other, he had to take the old homemade boat!"

13 THE THIEF AND THE SAINT
(Russia)

Long ago, a young rascal, named Yurig, lived in a certain village of a certain kingdom of Holy Russia and caused sorrow to everyone, especially his mother. For instead of earning an honest living like other youths—who plowed, planted and hilled beans for the farmers roundabout—Yurig lived by his wits. From boyhood he'd been light-fingered, sly and so cunning at thieving no one could catch him in the act. Nor did the Priest's warnings, the mutterings of the villagers or his mother's tears do any good. "Whether I do wrong or right makes no difference," Yurig complained with a show of innocence. "I get blamed for everything."

But the blame was not without justice. No one else in the village was so contemptible and mean. "When he strolls through the square on market days," the irate farmers declared, "a body must have eyes in the back of his head—if he's to keep the purse in his pocket, apples in his basket and cheeses from vanishing."

If the Priest found the poor box empty, after he'd seen the *Boyár*—a nobleman—drop in a ruble, or the youth's mother discovered the three kopecks she'd hoarded in the corner of her kerchief gone, they knew who the thief was. Yet accusations without proof never count. Besides, Yurig, who was cunning as a fox and slippery as an eel, never left evidence of his misdeeds.

120

When his widowed mother—who scrubbed for the rich folk from dawn to dark, in order to keep a few scraps and bits in the pot—upbraided her son for evil-doing and asked why he didn't work, he retorted, "Why should I when I get what I want without? But wait and see, dear Mother," he added, jingling the ill-gotten coins in his pocket. "One day, I'll be rich and take care of you."

"You'll end your days in jail!" his mother predicted. Then, throwing her apron over her face, she rocked back and forth, moaning in despair, "Dear Heaven, show me what to do."

But others predicted worse than jail for the young scallawag. "He'll end on the gallows," they muttered sourly and shook their fists. For what with the mysterious goings-on—the disappearance of fruit from orchards, eggs from under hens and freshly baked *pirogi*—little meat pies—from the housewives' shelves—folks were at their wits' end.

As time passed, things went from bad to worse. The hamlet buzzed with angry threats, his mother scolded and everyone shunned the youth. One day, when things got too hot for him, he decided to shake the dust of the village from his feet.

That's when Yurig first wandered from village to village, plying his evil trade as a thief and flourishing on the misfortune of others. "The world owes me a living," he said and took what he fancied, whether gold for his pocket or clothes for his back.

Since he was unknown in those parts, Yurig was able to play the part of a wolf in sheep's clothing. As he swaggered about, everyone took him for a young man of substance. And being good-looking, easy of manner and glib of tongue, he hoodwinked innkeepers, charmed the guests and always left a town better off than he came. "Why should a man work, when God gives him wits so he won't have to?" he chuckled, patting his pocket. Then he'd leave one town and hurry on to the next.

Yurig's wits sharpened with use. When he arrived at a place, he'd go to the inn, order the best room and the finest food and vodka. And what with his grand manner, the flash of gold and his habit of generous treating, everyone thought him a fine fellow—until the next day. By the time the innkeeper discovered his money gone, along with his guest, one customer reported his grandfather's gold watch missing and another his purse, the thief would be safely off with his loot. No matter how much commotion he caused, he always escaped. "No one will ever catch *me*," he boasted gleefully and laughed up his sleeve at the silly fools he had duped.

And no one did catch Yurig. Then one awful night, after almost three years, he made a mistake—a mistake that changed his whole life. That was the night he lodged in the village next the forest, attacked the Man with the Ring and discovered, too late, who he was.

Yurig, as usual, went to the inn, engaged the best room and sat down at a table with his vodka, to size up the other guests. He noticed at once the old man in the corner—the elegant clothes, the gold chain round his neck and the splendid ruby ring on the first finger of his white pudgy hand.

Aha, what a prize! Yurig thought, eyes glittering and fingers itching. Through half-closed lids he studied the ring, while others thought that he drowsed. The thief had never seen a gem of such deep glowing splendor or setting of such workmanship. In the dimly lighted low-raftered room, the ruby looked the color of pigeon blood. The longer the youth gazed at the ring, the more he wanted it and the more swiftly a wicked plan took shape in his mind.

From the manner in which the rustic louts, on entering the inn, bowed and scraped to the Man with the Ring, it was easy to tell he was someone important—doubtless a *Boyár*—Yurig decided. Only they could wear gems such as that! *Yet this very night, the ruby shall grace a younger hand,* he thought greedily. *While the rich* Boyár *lies somewhere on a dark road, I'll be far away with the ring."*

When the Man with the Ring left the inn, it was past midnight, the sky dark and the village asleep. But the thief, lurking in the bushes, wasn't asleep, and when the old man walked down the path and into the road, he followed stealthily. Moments later, when his victim turned into a lonely lane bordered by trees, Yurig was a few paces behind. Halfway up the lane, he struck the man, knocked him to the ground and then, thinking him unconscious, tried to twist off the ring from his forefinger. But the old fellow roused suddenly and with his last strength shouted, "Help! Help! A murderer—a thief has followed me." In the uproar that ensued, the youth dropped the old one's hand and tried to flee.

But escape seemed impossible. For all at once the entire village wakened, torches flared and feet came running. When Yurig heard shouts of "Quick! Quick! Our *Starósta's*—Mayor's—in trouble!" "Someone's attacked him," and "Don't let the thug get away," he knew there was no time to lose. The man he'd taken for the *Boyár*, was the *Starósta*, and now, with the inhabitants roused, the law would follow his attacker!

Yurig glanced about desperately. The angry shouts were closer, the footsteps running from every side. If the mob caught him, they'd drag him to the gallows and hang him at the crossroads.

Now torches flared at the end of the lane. As the crowd surged forward, Yurig plunged into the woods. With a bit of luck he'd be able to make his way to the next village, or so he thought, until the woods turned into a vast forest that seemed to lead nowhere. And now his plight was more desperate than before. For in the distance he could hear the pounding of horses' hooves and the threats of his pursuers coming from an old unused road.

How long Yurig fled through the vast forest, he didn't know. It might have been days or it might have been weeks. All he knew was that the faster he ran, the deeper the forest grew and the nearer the riders' shouts seemed. Like a hunted beast, he fled before them, crouched behind rocks and hid behind trees.

At last the horsemen fell behind and Yurig, who had reached the end of the forest, faced a new peril. For where the forest ended, the steppe began!

As Yurig stumbled, exhausted—bruised and so weary he could scarcely drag one foot after the other—he saw the vast treeless waste, at least nine versts broad and nine versts wide. Escape was impossible, for there was no shelter anywhere. Each instant the yelling horsemen were closer.

In his extremity, Yurig felt his lips moving. For the first time since childhood, he was praying. "Lord, forgive my sinful soul," he sobbed. "And you, dear Saint Nicholas, please hide me. If only you'll help, I'll burn a three-ruble candle before your image in church," he ended frantically.

The words had scarcely left his lips, when Yurig saw an old man with bent shoulders, long white beard and peasant tunic, who was gathering simples close by. "What was that you asked, young man?" asked the old one, glancing up sharply.

"I begged Saint Nicholas to hide me," said Yurig, with an apprehensive glance behind. "I'm a thief, I've sinned and repented. I—I promised the Saint a three-ruble candle, if only he'd hide me— but now it's too late," he concluded as shouts became more distinct.

"Hide in yonder pit," said the old man brusquely and pointed to a yawning hole Yurig hadn't noticed before. He had barely time to leap toward it—and crouch down among the half-gnawed bones inside —before the riders thundered from the forest.

Yurig choked and all but fainted from the noisomeness of the pit. But when he heard the horsemen shout, "Grandfather, have you seen the thief who fled this way?" and the old one's reply, he hugged himself in relief.

"A thief, eh?" crackled the aged man. "I'd see if a fly tried to escape across this barren waste!"

Yurig heard the riders gallop on. And now, though the foulness of the hole was stifling, he crouched there until, a lifetime later, they galloped back, entered the forest and the sound of hoofbeats died in the distance. Only when the steppe was still once more did he crawl from the pit. "Thank you, kind Grandfather," the youth cried. "You have saved my life."

"Hem—what was it you promised Saint Nicholas—if he'd hide you?" asked the old man.

For some reason Yurig was uneasy. "I promised to burn a candle before his image in church," he said.

"That's what I thought—so listen well, young man," thundered the old one, so sternly the thief blanched. "If you should burn a candle

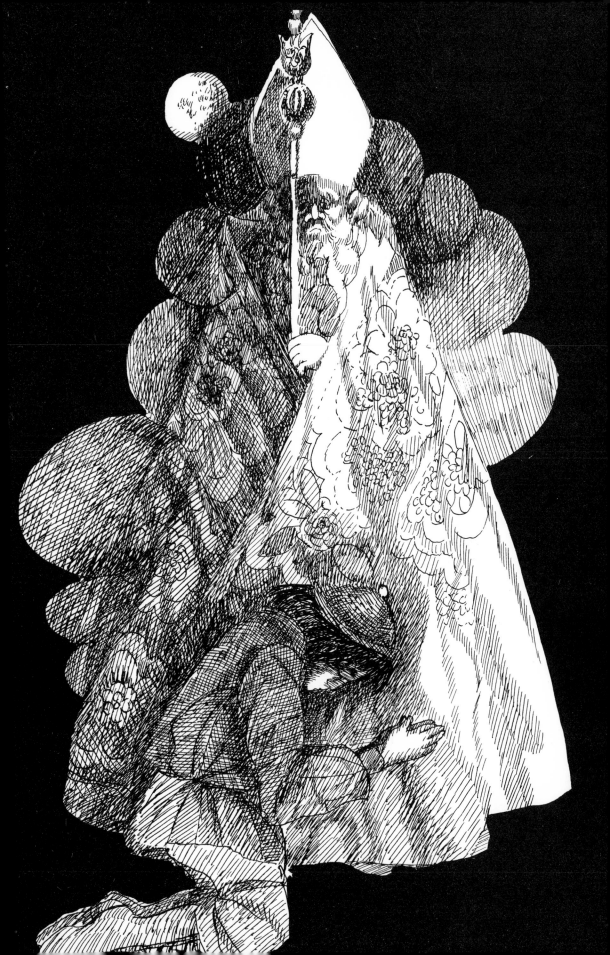

to Saint Nicholas, it would choke him, just as the stench of yonder pit choked you. Our Lord does not bless wicked deeds. Neither do his Saints protect evil-doers.''

The awful words spoken, the old man changed. He grew taller, his face shone like the sun and his eyes blazed. Shaking in terror, Yurig fell to his knees. For the instant he beheld the jeweled miter, the tall crook and the cope embroidered in golden thread, he knew he was looking at the Holy One himself. "You—you are Saint Nicholas!" he stammered. "I only meant to—to—"

"Bribe Saint Nicholas with a candle to save your own hide," said the Saint so scornfully Yurig quailed. "Only when there was nothing else to do did you pray Our Lord to forgive you and me to hide you."

Yurig hung his head in shame. For the first time in his evil life, he thought of how he'd cheated, stolen and caused grief to his mother and everyone else. Overcome with despair, his shoulders shook. He couldn't escape now—not with Christ and His Saints against him. He'd be hunted, caught and dragged to the gallows! "What can I do?" he moaned, face in hands.

"Return to your village, my son," replied Saint Nicholas, his voice suddenly gentle. "Warn others that Our Lord does not bless evil deeds—repent."

"But—but I don't know how," Yurig said miserably. "Besides, no one will trust me."

"If you heed my warning, people will—in time," encouraged the Saint, so kindly a faint hope stirred in the thief's breast. "Only when you repent in deed will Heaven bless you. And only then," he added with a faint smile, "burn your candle and ask Saint Nicholas to protect you."

The Saint had vanished when Yurig lifted his head. But the radiance that shone across the steppe gave him courage. Resolutely he turned his face homeward, and thus took the first step in his journey to grace.

"From that day, he was a changed man," say the Old Ones

who still tell the story of the Saint and the thief. "Yurig returned to his own village. There, in spite of mistrust and suspicion, he finally got work on a farm, supported his mother and earned an honest livelihood."

In time he also earned respect. For folks soon discovered that the young man who returned to the village was entirely different from the thief who'd run away. As he plowed, sowed and did chores for his Master, Yurig exhorted all who would listen, "Forsake evil deeds, pray for forgiveness and then ask Our Lord's blessing. And as for the Saints, ask them to protect you—if you repent from the heart."

Such was the power of the words of the man who'd once been a thief that many forsook their evil ways. "Your son is a second tongue to me," the Priest told the youth's mother.

The old woman smiled and smoothed her apron. "I always said my boy was good at heart," said she proudly.

After time passed—neither too much nor too little—the storytellers say that Yurig bought a fine expensive candle—one that cost three whole rubles! He took it to the onion-domed church, lighted the candle and burned it before the image of Saint Nicholas. Then the youth knelt, bowed his head and prayed humbly.

"And Saint Nicholas heard his prayers," the storytellers add. For though Yurig was never rich, he prospered. He took care of his mother until she died at a ripe old age. He married the prettiest girl in the village and finally bought a small farm of his own.

There the young couple lived happily and raised seven stalwart sons—the first, a fine bouncy lad with a merry laugh—was named Nicholas—after the Saint who helps all sinners.

The Author

DOROTHY GLADYS SPICER is a New Yorker, "since the early seventeenth century," she says, "when a Dutch sailmaker from Hoorn emigrated to New Amsterdam."

Miss Spicer was graduated from Vassar, and from Radcliffe, where she majored in art history and archeology. She is a folklorist, well known for her stories and work in peasant crafts and folk backgrounds. She has studied arts and native festivals in towns and villages of Europe and the Orient, where she has carried on special research under folklore experts of the various countries.

She now lives in White Plains, New York, and is author of many books and articles on folk festivals, customs, and foods. Included among her twenty-two books are *46 Days of Christmas, 13 Witches, 13 Monsters, 13 Ghosts, 13 Giants, 13 Devils, 13 Goblins* and *The Owl's Nest: Folktales from Friesland.*

398.2   Spicer, Dorothy
Spi
    13 jolly saints

DATE DUE			
FEB 3 '71			
FEB 10 '71			
MAR 8 '71			
APR 30			
Sep 29 '72			
Dec 3 '73			
Apr 22 '74			
Nov 4 '75			
Mar 28 '78			